The
PRINCESS DOLLS

LIBRARY AND ARCHIVES CANADA CATALOGUING IN PUBLICATION

Schwartz, Ellen, 1949-, author
The princess dolls / Ellen Schwartz ; illustrations by Mariko Ando.

Issued in print and electronic formats.
ISBN 978-1-926890-08-1 (hardcover).--ISBN 978-1-926890-29-6 (softcover)
ISBN 978-1-926890-49-4 (EPUB)

I. Ando, Mariko, illustrator II. Title.

PS8587.C578P45 2018   jC813'.54   C2017-907888-7
                                                        C2018-903613-3

Book design by Elisa Gutiérrez

The text of this book is set in Cassia • Title is set in Adorn Serif and Adorn Bouquet

10 9 8 7 6 5 4 3 2 1

Printed and bound in Canada on ancient-forest-friendly paper.

The publisher thanks Hilary Leung for her editorial help with this project.

The publisher thanks the Government of Canada, the Canada Council for the Arts and Livres Canada Books for their financial support. We also thank the Government of the Province of British Columbia for the financial support we have received through the Book Publishing Tax Credit program and the British Columbia Arts Council.

The PRINCESS DOLLS

❧ ELLEN SCHWARTZ ❧

illustrations by MARIKO ANDO

TRADEWIND BOOKS

Vancouver • London

In memory of my father—ES

For friendships everywhere—MA

• CONTENTS •

CHAPTER 1

*T*he doorbell rang.

"I'll get it!" Esther yelled. She clattered down the stairs and opened the door.

There on the doorstep stood three children. In the middle, Esther's best friend, Michiko. On one side, Michi's older brother, Tomo. On the other side, Michi's little sister, Akiko.

Esther gasped, staring at Michi. Not at Michi herself, but at what she was wearing.

A cape. It tied around her neck with a blue ribbon, flowed over the shoulders of her winter coat and fell in soft curves around her body. It was made of satiny material that shimmered in tones of silver, blue and rosy-pink.

"Oh, Michi!" Esther said, as Tomo squeezed past her, heading upstairs to Jake's room. "It's—it's *beautiful*! It's for Princess Margaret, isn't it?" At Michi's nod, Esther went on, "It's perfect. But where did you get it?"

Michiko smiled shyly. "I made it."

"You *made* it!" Esther repeated. "How?"

"Well, Mom was getting rid of this old worn-out dress, so I cut off the top, sewed a loop at the top of the skirt part and threaded a ribbon through it. Simple, really."

"Simple for you, maybe," Esther said with a laugh.

Akiko tugged on Esther's shirt. "I helped!"

"You did?" Esther bent down.

"Yup. I handed Michi *everything*. The thread and the needle and even the scissors."

"I bet you were a big help, Kiko."

Michi rolled her eyes. "When she stayed out of the way," she whispered.

Esther giggled.

Michi held the cape open. The inside was the darkest blue velvet, almost black. "You can wear it the satin side out or the velvet side out, Esther. Depending on whether Princess Margaret is going to a ball, or just for a stroll around Buckingham Palace."

Esther sighed. "Oh, Michi, I wish I had one for Princess Elizabeth. Then we could be princesses together."

Akiko wiggled. Michi elbowed her.

Esther looked from one sister to the other.

Michi grinned. Then she handed Esther a paper bag. Esther hadn't noticed it sitting on the doormat.

Esther drew out a cape—an identical cape—then looked at Michi in wonder.

Michi laughed. "Of course I made you one, silly. Two capes for two best friends. You are Princess Elizabeth and I am Princess Margaret."

Esther flung the cape over her shoulders. The velvet hugged her in a soft embrace. She threw her arms around Michi. "Thank you, thank you, thank you! Oh, Michi, it's beautiful. It's perfect." She struck a pose, one hand on her hip, the other raised in a royal wave. "Do I look like Princess Elizabeth?"

"You look like a goofy girl playing dress-up," said Jake, who had come downstairs with Tomo.

"Hey!"

He ducked out of the way as Esther went to smack him. "Come on, we'd better get moving, or we'll be late for the movie."

· · ·

The five children walked down Hastings Street toward the Pantages Theatre. Esther linked her arm through Michi's. "Shall we promena-a-a-ade through the palace, my dear sister Margaret?" she said in her best British accent.

"Yes, indeed, do let's, Elizabeth," Michi answered.

They walked arm in arm, taking slow, regal steps. Jake and Tomo moved ahead.

"I want to be a princess too," Akiko said.

"You can't," Michiko said. "We have only two princesses."

"But..." Akiko's lower lip wobbled.

"Tell you what, Kiko," Esther said. "You can hold up our capes, so they don't drag in the mud. Okay?"

"Okay!" Akiko skipped behind the two older girls, picked up the hem of each of their capes and followed along with slow steps. "I'm 'portant, aren't I?"

"Very 'portant," Esther assured her.

"Wasn't that a splendid ball last night, Margaret?" Esther asked, leaning toward Michi.

"Oh, yes, it was divine. And the refreshments, *so* delicious."

"Especially the champagne," Esther said with a grin.

"Esther! I mean, Elizabeth!"

Both girls dissolved in laughter.

Jake turned around. "Come on, slowpokes. We'll never get there at this rate."

"Bossy pants," Esther shouted back. But she didn't want to be late either. She turned to Michi. "Let's go horseback riding, Margaret."

They posed their hands in front of them, as if holding reins, then started galloping down the street.

"Wait for me!" Akiko cried.

Esther and Michiko each grabbed one of Akiko's arms and lifted her between them. Akiko shrieked with laughter. They galloped faster, tromping down the sidewalk until they caught up to Jake and Tomo.

"What on earth are you two doing?" Jake said.

Sticking her chin up, Esther said with as much dignity as she could muster, "We're royal princesses, riding our thoroughbreds, if you must know."

Jake and Tomo hooted with laughter. "More like stampeding elephants," Tomo said.

"Why, you—" Michi went for her brother, but he skipped out of the way.

"Pay no attention to those oafs, Margaret," Esther said, and they resumed their run.

As they pranced past Adachi's Shoes, Jimmy, a boy in their class at Strathcona School, came toward them. He pointed at Michi, Tomo and Akiko. "Go back to Japan!" he yelled.

The five children stood there, frozen.

Then Jake shouted, "They can't go *back*, dummy. They've never been there." Jimmy ran off. Esther, glancing at Michi's grim face, wished she had thought of saying that.

They walked on in silence. A moment later, though, when they came up to Rafelson's Toy Shop, Jimmy's words flew out of Esther's head. She stopped short.

The usual assortment of toys filled Rafelson's front window. Teddy bears and checkers games, building blocks and miniature tea sets, toy soldiers and paints. But today there was more.

Two dolls—two princesses—were propped on a platform high above the other toys. Each was about a foot tall. They stood upright, gazing out above the girls' heads.

Princess Elizabeth—it was *her* face exactly—wore tiny white gloves, shiny black pumps and a stylish powder-blue coat. Thick waves of real-looking brown hair curled around her porcelain face. A sparkling tiara crowned her head, and a faint smile tinged her red painted lips.

Next to her, Princess Margaret was dressed in a maroon cardigan over a ruffled white blouse and a navy, red and green plaid skirt. Circles of pink made her porcelain cheeks look rosy, and shiny black Mary Janes glinted on her feet.

"Oh, Michi..."

"Oh, Esther..."

They looked at one another, then turned the door handle.

"What do you think you're doing?" Jake asked. "We'll be late for the movie."

"Tomo, take Akiko," Michi said, thrusting her sister at her brother. Before he could protest, she and Esther slipped inside.

Mr Rafelson was stacking model-airplane kits on a shelf. "Good afternoon, Esther and Michiko. What can I do for you girls?"

"The dolls. The princess dolls..."

Mr Rafelson smiled. "Yes, they are wonderful, aren't they?"

"How... how much?"

"Fifteen dollars."

"Each?" Michi squeaked.

Mr Rafelson nodded.

Esther gasped. "So much!"

"I know it's a lot. But the dolls came all the way from England, you see."

Esther leaned close to Michi. "Our birthdays are coming up."

Esther and Michi had been born on the same day, February 7, 1933. That was how their families had met and become friends.

"But Mom and Dad could never..." Michi didn't finish.

"There's got to be a way," Esther said. But even as she said it, she knew it was impossible. The princess dolls were way too expensive.

But if only…

Jake and Tomo poked their heads through the doorway. "Come *on*!" Jake said.

He grabbed Esther's hand, Tomo grabbed Michi's, and Michi grabbed Akiko's. In a raggedy line, they ran the rest of the way to the cinema.

CHAPTER TWO

*E*sther and Michi leaned close together, nibbling popcorn. Akiko sat on the other side of Michi, Tomo and Jake next to her.

The screen lit up. WORLD NEWS: JANUARY 12, 1942. "First, news from the war in the Pacific," the announcer said in a solemn voice. "One month after the attack on the United States Naval Station in Pearl Harbor, the Japanese Army continues its march through Southeast Asia, conquering every country in its path."

On the screen, hundreds of Japanese soldiers marched in precise formation. Their metal helmets glinted in the light, and their knees drilled up and down like pistons.

The audience hissed.

Michi flinched, and popcorn scattered from her hand.

"However, over in Europe," the announcer went on, "the Royal Air Force made successful bombing runs on Hamburg."

The image on the screen changed. Two flyers stepped out of a de Havilland Mosquito bomber, looking haggard but smiling.

Esther and Michi and their brothers cheered, along with the audience.

"Meanwhile in Britain, as the Blitz rages on," the announcer said, "the Royal Family is encouraging all British subjects to fight with pride and courage."

On the screen, King George and Queen Elizabeth stood on a balcony at Buckingham Palace, flanked by Princesses Elizabeth and Margaret. They all waved, turning their hands slowly back and forth. Below, the crowd cheered and fluttered British flags.

Esther squeezed Michiko's hand.

The scene changed to the inside of a warehouse. The announcer said, "Princess Elizabeth and Princess Margaret are assisting in the war effort." The camera zoomed in on the two sisters, who folded blankets and placed them on a pile.

"Michi," Akiko said, "what are they doing?"

"Shush!" Michi hissed.

A reporter held a microphone up to Princess Elizabeth. "Don't you get tired, Your Highness?"

Elizabeth smiled shyly. "Sometimes. But Margaret and I need to do our part for our loyal troops."

"If we all pitch in together, we're sure to win the war," Princess Margaret added.

They went back to folding blankets.

Esther sighed. Even dressed in a plain sweater set and pleated skirt, Elizabeth looked regal. And she was so brave! She and Margaret had stayed in London, despite the Blitz.

"Margaret and I need to do our part for our loyal troops," she whispered to herself, copying Elizabeth's accent exactly.

With a flourish of music, the newsreel ended, and *Dumbo*, the feature, started. Esther loved the adventures of the clumsy baby elephant with the enormous ears. But as she watched, part of her was back at Buckingham Palace, seeing Princess Elizabeth raise her graceful hand to wave, over and over.

• • •

On the way home, the five children stopped at Suzuki's Store, the corner store that Michi's parents ran. Esther was surprised to see a small crowd of people gathered out front. But as she drew closer she realized that the people weren't going in—they were just standing there.

Then she spotted two of her classmates, Florence and Trudy, among the group. They were pointing at something on the door.

"What's going on?" Tomo said.

Esther pushed forward. Taped to the front door of Suzuki's Store was a crude cartoon. It showed a buck-toothed Japanese soldier raising a sabre, dripping with blood.

"What is it, Michi?" Akiko asked.

"Nothing," Michi said, angrily tearing the drawing down.

Esther heard Florence and Trudy snickering. She turned around. "It's not funny!"

Florence tossed her head. "Yes, it is. Besides, the Japanese are our enemies, so who cares about a cartoon, anyway?"

"Why did she say that?" Akiko asked. "We're not enemies."

"Of course not, Kiko. Ignore her," Esther said, taking Akiko's hand.

Florence began, "They kill—"

"Stop it!" Esther stomped her foot. Florence and Trudy scampered away.

Michi crumpled the drawing in her hand. "I will never ever speak to Florence again," she said bitterly.

The five children filed into the store. Uncle Ted was stocking shelves, and Aunt Fumiko was behind the cash register.

To Esther, Michi's parents were Aunt Fumiko and Uncle Ted. Michi called Esther's parents Aunt Gladdy and Uncle Herbie.

Uncle Ted looked up. "What was all that fuss outside?"

Michi flattened the cartoon and showed it to her father.

"Another one?" Aunt Fumiko asked in a low voice.

Uncle Ted nodded. He and his wife exchanged a worried look.

"What is it, Daddy?" Akiko asked. "Michi wouldn't show me."

"Nothing you need to see, Kiko." He put the paper in his pocket, then lifted her into his arms. "Now, tell me," he said in a hearty voice, "how was the movie?"

"Oh, it was so good, Daddy!" Akiko said. "Dumbo was funny when he flew with his big ears. Only I cried when the mean man sent his mama away."

"She wasn't the only one," Tomo told his father. "Michi cried too."

"So did you!" Michi said. "I saw. Right, Esther?"

Esther nodded. "And Jake."

"We did not!" Jake said.

Uncle Ted winked at Esther. "Tough guys, eh?"

Fingering a penny in her pocket, Esther went to the candy counter and gazed at the jars of brightly coloured jawbreakers. Licorice was her favourite flavour—she didn't even mind when Jake teased her about her black teeth—but the lemon yellow was so bright and golden, and the cherry red looked delicious too. Finally, handing over her penny, she said, "One black, Aunt Fumiko, please."

Aunt Fumiko slipped a red into the bag too.

"Thanks!"

Esther and Jake said goodbye, leaving their friends at the store. As they walked down the street, Esther, her cheek bulging, said, "I bet it was Mr Harper who put up that drawing."

Jake turned to her in surprise. "Our neighbour Mr Harper? Why do you think that?"

"The other day, when Tomo threw his newspaper onto the front step, he shook his fist and called Tomo a dirty name."

They walked the rest of the way home in silence, the licorice melting on Esther's tongue.

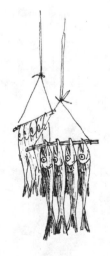

CHAPTER 3

$\mathcal{E}$very few days Esther and Michi stopped in at Rafelson's. So far the dolls were still there.

One day in late January they ran to the store straight from school.

"Hello, girls. Come to check on the dolls?" Mr Rafelson asked.

Esther gripped the counter. "Has anyone…" She couldn't finish.

He nodded. "Yes, a few people have asked about them. A granny was in yesterday, looking for something for her granddaughter. She nearly took the dolls, but chose a crocheting kit instead."

"Poor kid," Esther said under her breath. She shot Michi a smile.

• • •

A few days later, they checked again.

"A father came in just today, looking for gifts for his twin girls," Mr Rafelson said.

Twins! Esther thought with alarm. *One princess doll for each girl.*

"But the price was too dear," Mr Rafelson said.

"Whew!" Esther said. But that was little comfort. The price was just as out of reach for *them* as it was for the father of the twins.

• • •

When she got home, Esther went straight to the kitchen. Her mother was busy arranging cinnamon rolls on a baking tray. She baked pastries and donated them to the Red Cross, who sold them to raise money for the war effort. Sprinkles of cinnamon dusted the counter, filling the kitchen with a spicy smell.

Esther dipped her finger in a bowl of cinnamon sugar and licked it. "Mama, I don't suppose you've been by Rafelson's lately?"

Her mother gave her a curious look. "No, why?"

"Well . . . they have these new dolls. Princess Elizabeth and Princess Margaret. And they're beautiful, Mama. You really should see them."

"I should, should I?"

"Yes. They're really well made. They have china heads and cloth bodies, and their clothes are exactly like what the real princesses wear. And I was thinking . . ."

Her mother slid the tray into the oven. "Yes?"

"Well, my birthday's coming soon, and the Princess Elizabeth doll would make such a swell present. And if Michi got the Princess Margaret doll, it would be just perfect."

"I see you've got it all figured out."

"Yup!" Esther said with a grin. This was going much better than she'd dared hope.

"I suppose they're frightfully expensive," her mother said, filling the sink with sudsy water.

"Well, yes, they are, but—"

Her mother dried her hands and put her arm around Esther. "Don't get your hopes up, sweetheart. Daddy and I are trying to save our pennies these days."

Esther's shoulders slumped. "Okay, Mama. But if you saw the doll, I know you'd change your mind."

Her mother didn't answer. Esther went up to her room and flopped onto her bed with a sigh.

• • •

The next day Michi reported that she'd had no luck either.

"I promised I'd do extra chores if they got me the Princess Margaret doll, like give Akiko her bath, do Tomo's share of the dishes while he's out delivering papers and put away the groceries. But Mom pointed out that I have to do those things anyway."

"Rats."

Michiko sighed glumly.

Esther thought for a minute, then said, "Don't give up. Send thoughts into their heads. 'You will buy me the doll...you will buy me the doll...'"

Michi laughed. "You mean hypnotize them?"

"Don't laugh. It could work." *It's the only thing that might work,* she thought.

· · ·

A few days later, Esther had another idea. She cleaned off her dresser, shoving a mound of stuffed animals, a shoebox full of pencil crayons, a lone mitten and her piggy bank, sadly empty, into her closet. She ran downstairs.

"Mama, guess what I just did."

Today her mother was making hot cross buns. "What?"

"I cleaned off my dresser. Don't you think the Princess Elizabeth doll would look good there?"

"Esther, I told you—"

"I know, I know. But I promise I'll keep my room as neat as a pin forever and ever if you get me the doll."

Turning the dough over with a quick flick of the wrist, her mother smiled. "Forever and ever?"

"Yes, really! You know why?"

"Why?"

"Because Princess Elizabeth will set such a good example, I'll just *have* to follow it. You won't believe how good I'll be."

Her mother sprinkled a handful of currants over the dough. "You're right. I won't believe it."

"Mama!"

"Esther, I know you love Princess Elizabeth and that you're pining for the doll. But I just don't think it's possible."

Esther's face fell. She headed out of the kitchen.

"Esther?"

She turned back. "Yeah?"

"I bet your dresser looks much better."

"Mama!"

• • •

Wearing their capes, Esther and Michiko paraded up and down Esther's room. There was only a week to go before their birthdays, and the dolls were as far out of reach as ever.

Esther heard the doorbell ring. A moment later, her mother called, "Esther! Mail for you."

Esther flew downstairs, then back up. "It's from Grandma Sadie." She carefully opened the flap and pulled out a letter. "Oh, guess what, Michi! She's coming for my birthday! For *our* birthdays. She's taking the train all the way from Toronto."

"Swell!" Michi loved Esther's grandmother—everyone did.

Esther emptied the envelope. "Goody, more pictures." Every few weeks, Grandma Sadie sent Esther photographs

she had clipped from magazines. Especially pictures of Princess Elizabeth, Esther's favourite.

Esther spread out the photos on her bed. One, titled "School Days at the Palace," showed Princess Elizabeth and Princess Margaret in their school uniforms, every pleat in their plaid skirts lying just so, books clutched to their chests.

In another, the princesses frolicked in the garden with their corgis. Two little bundles of brown and white fur jumped in the air.

"Look how adorable Dookie and Jane are," Esther said, pointing to the dogs' sticking-up ears.

A third picture showed Princess Margaret standing at the top of a marble staircase, wearing a forest-green dress with a thin white belt and a white Peter Pan collar. Her perfectly waved hair just touched her shoulders.

"Here, Michi. You have this one."

Michi reached out her hand, but didn't take the picture. "Don't you want it for your collection?"

"It's all right. I have so many."

Michi's face turned a faint pink. "Thanks."

Together they taped up the rest of the new pictures, then stood back to admire Esther's gallery. The princesses in ball gowns and dressing gowns and sweater sets; the princesses drinking tea and picking flowers and riding horses; the princesses at their desks and in boats and in open-topped cars.

Esther sighed.

Michi sighed.

"We've got to get those dolls."

"Yes, but how?"

"We'll think of something."

Both girls looked at the calendar on Esther's wall. The days were ticking by. And neither set of parents had shown the slightest sign of splurging on the dolls.

CHAPTER 4

"Grandma Sadie!" Esther cried, flinging herself into her grandmother's arms.

It was February sixth, the day before her birthday, and Daddy had just picked up Grandma Sadie from the train station.

Esther burrowed into the soft mink collar of Grandma Sadie's coat. She sniffed. Yes, there was her grandmother's familiar lilac perfume.

Grandma Sadie unfastened her coat buttons. Esther waited for her to place the coat in her arms, wink and say, "Put this upstairs for me, darlink?" like she always did. Esther always put the coat on and posed in front of the mirror like a fancy lady.

But Grandma Sadie didn't wink. She didn't say anything. She sat down at the kitchen table and rested her chin on her hand.

Esther waited some more. Finally, she said, "Want me to put your coat upstairs for you, Grandma?"

Grandma Sadie blinked. "Of course. I forgot. Here you go, Estherle."

Carrying the coat upstairs, Esther thought, *Grandma Sadie must be tired. After all, it's a long trip on the train.*

That evening at dinner, Grandma Sadie was quiet. Normally she ate big portions of Mama's cooking and told Mama how delicious it was, but tonight she barely ate. There was a strange look on her face, as if her thoughts were elsewhere.

When she put her fork down and sighed, Daddy said, "Mama? You all right?"

Grandma Sadie nodded slowly. "Fine, Herbie, fine."

Esther saw Mama and Daddy exchange a look.

After dinner, Esther and Jake went into the living room. They waited by the piano for Grandma Sadie to come in.

She didn't.

When Esther went to check, Grandma Sadie was still sitting at the kitchen table, talking in a low voice with Mama and Daddy.

"Grandma?" Esther said. "Aren't you going to play piano with us?"

Grandma Sadie couldn't really play the piano. Whenever she visited, she sat on the piano stool with Esther on one side and Jake on the other. She crashed her hands on the piano keys, down in the low notes, up in the high notes, down and up, down and up, singing "La-la-la-la-la," pretending to be a great opera singer.

"I'm sorry, sweetheart. I'm just not in the mood."

"How about cards?" Esther said.

Every year, Grandma Sadie taught Esther a new card game. Last year, when she turned eight, Grandma Sadie had taught her how to play Hearts. Esther even beat her once—and Grandma Sadie didn't let you win. Ever.

Grandma Sadie shook her head. "Not tonight, *mommie-shainee*. In fact, I think I'll turn in."

She rose, kissed Esther and Jake, then went upstairs.

Jake took Esther aside. "Something's wrong."

• • •

The next morning, Esther felt a little shiver when she remembered that it was her birthday. She put on her party dress. It was her High Holidays dress from the Jewish New

Year in the fall, a sailor dress with a wide white collar, pale blue and white stripes, and a jaunty red bow at the neck.

She was debating whether to knock on Grandma Sadie's door when her grandmother came out.

"Happy birthday, Estherle," Grandma Sadie said.

"Thanks, Grandma," Esther said. She held out her arms to show Grandma Sadie her dress. She waited.

Normally Grandma Sadie would clutch her heart and pretend to swoon, exclaiming, "*Oy vey*, so beautiful!" She would beckon Esther into her room and spray her with a spritz of her special lilac perfume, and maybe even let Esther put on a dab of her scarlet lipstick.

But today Grandma Sadie didn't do any of those things. She just said, "Very pretty," and started down the stairs.

Disappointed and puzzled, Esther followed her. *Jake's right*, she thought. *Something is wrong*.

But she had no time to think about it, because she had to help Mama stack napkins and forks and plates on the dining room table. Every year, she and Michi celebrated their birthdays together, taking turns having a party at one or the other of their houses. This year it was Esther's turn.

The doorbell rang. When Esther opened the door, rain blew in on a gust of wind, and she jumped back with a laugh. Michi, Akiko, Tomo and Aunt Fumiko stood on the doorstep.

"Happy birthday, Esther!"

"Happy birthday, Michi!"

Jake came to the door to greet Tomo. "Let's go upstairs and get away from these girls," he said.

"You're not invited anyway," Esther said with a toss of her head.

"Until it's time for cake," Jake said with a smirk.

"Happy birthday, Esther," Aunt Fumiko said, leaning forward to kiss Esther on the cheek. She laughed. "My goodness, you're getting so tall, I hardly need to bend down anymore." She took Akiko's hand. "Come in the kitchen with me."

Akiko pulled her hand away. "I want to stay with the big girls."

"Kiko, go with Mom," Michi said.

Akiko stuck her lip out, giving Esther a piteous look.

Esther leaned close to Michi. "I don't mind."

Michi rolled her eyes. "You always fall for it, Esther."

"Yay!" Akiko said, tears forgotten.

Carrying a plate covered with a cloth napkin, Aunt Fumiko went into the kitchen to help Mama get ready. Esther and Michi put their presents for each other on the coffee table in the living room. Esther's gift to Michi was round, about the size of a 78 record, but soft in the middle. Esther had used a great deal of wrapping paper, folding it over and over around the circle. There was a large lump of tape where the points met in the centre.

Michi shook the present. No noise. "Hmm, what could this possibly be?"

"Not telling."

Esther lifted Michi's present to her. It was square, about the size of a book. But when she squeezed it, it felt soft. She lifted an eyebrow.

"I know what it is!" Akiko said. "I saw Michi—"

Michi clapped a hand over her sister's mouth. "And you're not telling, are you?"

Akiko shook her head, eyes wide.

The doorbell rang, and girls started coming in. Ella and Doris, best friends like Esther and Michi, in matching red wool berets. Noriko, with two ruler-straight braids. Yoko, her eyeglasses sprinkled with raindrops.

Esther and Michi greeted them and put their presents on the coffee table.

The doorbell blared three times.

"Heavens, someone's impatient," Aunt Fumiko said, coming into the living room.

Esther opened the door. In marched Florence, trailed by Trudy.

"Happy birthday, you two," Florence trilled. She twirled around as if in excitement, but Esther knew it was really

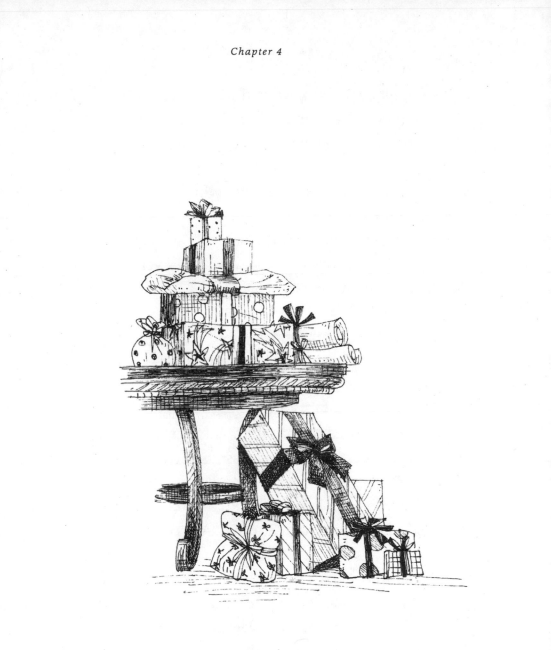

to show off her dress. It was red velvet, with a full skirt and a satin bow in back, and a short quilted jacket that closed with velvet-covered buttons. A matching red bow held back her golden curls.

Michi turned to Esther and whispered, "What's *she* doing here?"

Esther gave her a sheepish look. "Mama made me invite her, 'cause she invited me to her party last year."

"I don't care. I don't want her."

"Michi—"

But Michi had turned away, and Esther had to leave it so she could usher the girls into the living room to play charades.

Ella went first. She signed that she was going to act out a song, then pointed her finger as if at a distant target.

"The kitchen?" Esther guessed. "Something in the kitchen?"

"What's she doing, Michi?" Akiko said.

"Acting something out. Be quiet, Akiko."

"But—"

Esther took Akiko's hand. "Just watch," she whispered.

Ella pointed harder as if to suggest something farther away. She had long arms and legs, and when she stretched her body, she reminded Esther of a stork. *A very nice, graceful stork*, she told herself.

"Go away?" Florence said.

"Get lost?" Yoko said.

Everyone gave up. Laughing, Ella said, "'Over There.'"

"Oh, I get it," Doris said. "Nice try, Elephant."

The girls giggled. That was Doris' nickname for Ella. It was funny, since Ella was tall and thin. Ella called Doris "Dolittle," after the doctor, since she loved animals and was always bringing home strays.

Then Esther got "God Save the King." For the first word, she raised her arms as if to heaven, looking upward.

"Sky?" Noriko guessed.

"Clouds?" Ella said.

Shaking her head, Esther signalled that she would attempt the second word. She flailed around as if drowning, then raised one hand "above the water," as if pleading for help.

"You're funny, Esther," Akiko said with a giggle.

Esther flailed around some more, thrusting her hand higher.

"You're drowning," Michi said.

Esther nodded vigorously.

"Drowning... help... help me... save me..."

Esther raised her arms heavenward again, then repeated the saving motion.

"God!" Michi said. "God save me... 'God Save the King!'"

"Yes!" Esther shouted. "You're so smart, Michi."

"You're good at drowning," Michi said with a grin.

"I knew that. I was just about to call it out," Florence said, pouting. "Not fair, Michiko."

Michi scowled.

"Now, Florence, Michi got it fair and square," Mama said.

Florence huffed, but didn't say anything more. Trudy patted her hand sympathetically.

The mothers arranged the girls around the dining room table. Singing "Happy Birthday," they carried in two plates—Mama's vanilla cupcakes with chocolate icing and Aunt Fumiko's pale green teacakes.

Jake and Tomo, who had snuck into the dining room, sang, "Happy birthday to you, you belong in a zoo, you look like a monkey, and you act like one too."

"You should talk, you baboon," Esther said, though she and Michi couldn't help laughing as their brothers pranced around like monkeys, hands tucked in their armpits.

One cupcake and one teacake had candles in them. Before she and Michi blew them out together, Esther closed her eyes. *I wish Michi and I could be best friends forever.*

"You make the best cupcakes, Mrs Shulman," Florence said, taking a dainty bite.

"Thank you, dear."

"That's why I always gain five pounds whenever I come here," Grandma Sadie said. She was sitting on the couch with a plate on her lap.

Esther giggled. It was true. Grandma Sadie never could resist Mama's baking. Neither could Daddy. That was why they were both plump. Mama, despite all her baking, stayed slim.

When the teacakes came around, Florence passed the plate on without taking one. "No thank you," she said loudly. She leaned close to Trudy. Esther heard her whisper, "I'm not eating any Japanese cakes."

"Florence!" Esther said. She glanced around. Only she and Michi seemed to have heard. She took her best friend's hand under the table and squeezed it. Michi's face was like stone.

Now she's really mad, Esther thought. *She'll never forgive Florence.*

"This teacake is delicious, Aunt Fumiko," Esther said. And it was too. Aunt Fumiko's teacakes were delicate and round, like miniature cakes, not as sweet as regular cake, with a mild taste of green tea. "Can I have another one?"

"Of course," Aunt Fumiko said, smiling with pleasure. "Anyone else?"

"Me!" Jake said.

"Me too," said Tomo.

For once, Esther was glad Jake and Tomo were there.

"Time for presents," Mama announced, and the girls trooped into the living room, sitting in a circle on the floor.

Most of them had got Esther and Michi identical gifts: two pencil cases, two books, two sets of jacks, two yo-yos.

"Open mine," Florence said. It was lacy handkerchiefs, yellow for Esther, pink for Michiko.

"Oh, Florence, you always pick the prettiest things," Trudy said.

Esther poked Michiko with the slightest pressure. A lace handkerchief! You couldn't even blow your nose on it. Michi snorted, then covered it up with a cough.

Michi's eyes grew wide when she opened Esther's present: a set of embroidery hoops with a packet of needles and several skeins of thread in red, purple, green, blue and gold. Michi fanned out the colours, a rainbow in her hand. "Thanks," she said softly. Esther knew that that quiet voice meant she really liked the gift.

Esther picked up Michi's gift to her. "It's got to be a book," she said, feeling its shape again, and it was. An autograph book. Michi had sewn a cloth cover over the regular cover, and embroidered "Esther's Autographs" in fancy writing. On the flyleaf she had inscribed:

North, south, east, west,
You're the friend I love the best.

"Oh, Michi, I love it!" Esther threw her arms around her best friend.

"I knew!" Akiko cried. "And I didn't tell!"

"I would have killed you if you had," Michi said, laughing.

Grandma Sadie came in, carrying a large box.

"What's this?" Esther asked.

"One more gift, from me."

The box was covered in Rafelson's wrapping paper, blue with yellow balloons. A crazy thought flashed through Esther's mind. It was the right size. And shape. And weight.

But it couldn't be... could it?

She tore open the paper, hardly daring to breathe.

It was.

Princess Elizabeth! The tiara sparkled. Her eyes were closed, since she was lying flat, and a long fringe of eyelashes rested on her pink porcelain cheeks. The tiny white gloves on her tiny hands were fastened with a tiny pearl.

"What is it, what is it?" Akiko said, squirming closer. Then, "Michi, look!"

"Oh," Michi said in a strange voice.

Esther lifted the doll out of the box. Princess Elizabeth's eyes opened, and she looked at Esther with a warm brown gaze that seemed to say *I'm yours.*

"Oh—oh—Grandma Sadie—I can't believe it!" Cradling the doll in her arm, Esther jumped up and gave her grandmother a hug. She whipped around, holding the doll in front of her. "Look, everybody. It's Princess Elizabeth. Isn't she the most beautiful thing you've ever seen?"

The girls crowded around, forming a tight circle around Esther, blocking out Michi.

"Phooey," Florence said. "My mother was going to get me both princess dolls for my birthday. That way you wouldn't break up the set. And I have the most perfect dollhouse they could stay in."

"It's true," Trudy said. "Florence's dollhouse is amazing."

"Like a *palace*," Florence said.

Esther ignored her. She dropped a deep curtsey, holding Princess Elizabeth in front of her. "You are all my loyal subjects, and I am dee-lighted to see you here today," she said in a British accent.

Yoko giggled. "We are honoured to be invited, Your Majesty."

Esther gently pulled up one of the princess' arms. "Look, her arms move!" She raised the arm all the way up. "I'm giving you the royal wave." She waved at each girl around the circle.

"I feel all shivery, just as if the real princess was waving at me," Ella said.

"Oh, look at her sweet little shoes," Doris said.

"And look—the tiara comes off!" Esther said, gently removing it, then putting it back.

"Can I feel her hair?" Noriko asked.

"Yes, but be careful," Esther said, holding out the doll but keeping her arm around it.

Noriko stroked a curl. "It feels real."

"I bet it is," Esther said. "They wouldn't use fake hair for Princess Elizabeth."

"Well, I suppose that if I get the Princess Margaret doll, we can play together, Esther," Florence said. "I would let you use my tea set. It's real china, you know."

"There's nothing Princess Elizabeth would like better than having tea with Princess Margaret," Esther said with a laugh. She held up a pretend teacup. "Pinkies out, of course!"

"Say, Esther, could I hold her?" Doris asked. "Just for a second?"

"Sure, you all can," Esther said, feeling generous. "For a second."

She held out the doll and Doris carefully took her in her arms. Eyes wide, she gazed down at the doll as if it were a fragile baby. "Oh-h-h…" was all she said.

A hush fell over the group as the doll was passed from arm to arm. Yoko's face turned red. Trudy lay the doll down so her eyes closed. Noriko touched the tiny button on her shoes. Ella stroked her blue coat. Florence smoothed a finger over the tiara and tapped the nail polish on each finger.

Esther stretched out her arms. "That's enough, Florence. After all, I'm not giving her to you." She gave a nervous laugh.

Florence handed the doll back. Esther held her tight.

"I'm so glad you like my gift, sweetheart," Grandma Sadie said.

"*Like* it? I love it!"

Akiko squeezed into the circle. "Can I see, Esther?"

"Kiko!" Esther said—and suddenly she remembered. Michi. She'd forgotten all about her best friend. Where was Michi anyway?

She turned and looked behind her.

Michi was sitting there, holding the embroidery set, a smile fixed on her face, a sheen of tears in her eyes.

Instantly, Esther felt terrible. She went over to her friend. "Michi, I . . ." She trailed off. What should she say?

"Michi," she said again, trying to find the right words.

The doorbell rang.

"I didn't know . . . I mean, I wish . . ."

Michi looked away.

"Esther," Mama called, "Noriko's mother is here. Would you please get her coat?"

With a desperate look at Michi, Esther tore herself away. Then more mothers came, and Esther had to find those friends' coats too, and thank them and say goodbye. And then stack up all her presents and collect the cards. Somehow, before she knew it, Michi was giving her a stiff hug and saying, "Thank you for the gift, Esther," and then she and Akiko and Tomo and Aunt Fumiko were gone.

• • •

That night, as she got into bed, Esther's stomach hurt. "Too much cake," Mama said. But Esther knew it wasn't that. Not entirely that.

She and Michi had never argued before. Well, they weren't really arguing now. But the expression on Michi's face, so hurt and upset, and the cold way she'd said goodbye, made Esther feel worse than if they had been.

Michi's jealous, she thought. *That's why she acted like that.*

Esther couldn't blame her. She'd have been jealous too if Michi had got the Princess Margaret doll and Esther hadn't got Princess Elizabeth.

But she knew it wasn't only jealousy. It was—her stomach clenched and she forced herself to admit it—that she had ignored Michi. She hadn't meant to, but the other girls had gathered around her and she'd got so carried away showing them the doll that she'd forgotten all about Michi.

"It's not my fault I got the doll," she said aloud. "And you didn't have to act like that, Michi. I don't know why you got so mad."

A thought came.

Michi was really upset when Florence made that remark about the Japanese teacakes.

But then again, maybe it was when Florence said that if she got the Princess Margaret doll, we could play dolls together, and I said Princess Elizabeth would love to have tea with Princess Margaret.

Esther laughed. "It can't be that. You can't seriously think I'd want to play dolls with Florence!"

But if it *was* that, then it was all just a silly mis-understanding. Easily fixed.

I'll go over tomorrow and explain, Esther thought. *And I'll let Michi play with Princess Elizabeth, as much as she wants. And she'll be so happy that she'll get over it, and everything'll go back the way it was.*

Esther gave a relieved sigh. Her stomach unclenched.

Now she could enjoy her doll. She lifted Princess Elizabeth, and the doll's eyes flew open. Esther walked her across her pillow. She dipped the doll as if she were curtseying. She raised one arm, the other, lowered them. Princess Elizabeth gazed out regally. There was a tiny hole in the centre of her red lips, as if she were about to speak.

"Happy birthday, Esther," Esther whispered in the princess' voice. "I am so glad I'm yours."

Two minutes later, she was asleep, Princess Elizabeth cradled in her arms.

CHAPTER 5

*A*s soon as Esther woke up, her eyes lit on the Princess Elizabeth doll lying next to her on the pillow. "Hello! Good morning! You're mine!" she said aloud, and laughed.

Then she remembered Michi, and her plan to let Michi play with the doll. She'd go over right after breakfast. Michi would be thrilled, and everything would be fine.

Downstairs, Grandma Sadie was at the kitchen table with Mama and Daddy, and they were deep in conversation. When Esther came in, the talk broke off. Grandma Sadie had that same worried look on her face, and she was twisting a ring around and around her finger.

"What's going on?" Esther asked.

Mama fixed her a bowl of cereal. "Nothing you need to worry about, sweetheart. But would you take this in the living room, please?"

Eat in the living room? Normally that wasn't allowed. *This must be serious.*

Esther sat on the end of the couch closest to the kitchen. She strained to hear but could make out only the occasional word: "... not like her ... such a long silence ..."

What could it possibly be about?

Jake came in with his own bowl of cereal. Esther leaned close. "Jake, what are they talking about?"

He shrugged. "I don't know exactly. Something about Aunt Anna."

"Grandma Sadie's sister?"

Jake nodded.

"What about her?"

"All I know is that Grandma Sadie hasn't heard from her in a long time, and she's worried."

Esther had never met Aunt Anna, but she knew a few things about her from Grandma Sadie: that Aunt Anna was five years older than Grandma Sadie; that when Grandma Sadie had come to Canada many years earlier, Aunt Anna and her husband, Uncle Josef, had stayed in Germany; and that Aunt Anna was a brilliant mathematician and a talented musician. "She can really play the piano, not like me," Grandma Sadie had told Esther, laughing.

"What does Grandma Sadie think happened to her?" Esther asked.

Jake shrugged. "I don't think anyone knows."

Voices drifted in from the kitchen. "... over a year ... safe haven ..."

Esther and Jake exchanged a look. Without saying a word, they tiptoed over to the kitchen door and flattened themselves behind the doorframe.

"They may have tried to get out of Germany," Grandma Sadie was saying. "But I have no idea. Oh, I wish she would get in touch!"

"She's probably tried," Daddy said. "But you know how impossible it is getting word out during wartime. I'm sure once she gets to a safe place, she'll write."

"But what if it's too late?" Grandma Sadie cried. "I've heard that the Nazis are rounding up Jews and sending them to work camps—"

Esther's eyes opened wide. Jake shot her an alarmed look.

"Now, Mama, don't get ahead of yourself," Daddy said. "It's just a rumour at this point."

"So you've heard about this, Herbie?" Mama said.

There was a pause. "Well, yes, the *Messenger*'s foreign correspondent just came back from Britain. He heard whispers about these camps." When Grandma Sadie moaned, he added quickly, "But we don't know for sure. So let's hope for the best."

"I'm sure Anna and Josef are okay," Mama said in a soothing voice.

Grandma Sadie murmured something that Esther couldn't hear. Just as she leaned closer to the doorway, there was the sound of a chair being pushed back. Esther and Jake sprang for the couch.

Too late.

Mama came in. She wagged her finger. "You rascals."

"Are Aunt Anna and Uncle Josef going to be okay, Mama?" Esther asked.

Mama looked sharply at them. "What did you hear?"

"Just that Grandma Sadie hasn't heard from Aunt Anna and doesn't know where she is."

"And that they may be trying to get out of Germany," Jake added.

Mama paused as if weighing her words. "Well, that's about it. But Daddy's going to make some inquiries at the newspaper, see what he can find out." She put on a smile. "And no news is good news, right?"

It was a question that didn't seem to need an answer.

CHAPTER 6

With Princess Elizabeth cradled in her arms, Esther rang Michi's doorbell.

"Esther!" Aunt Fumiko said. "Oh, look how lovely." She bent over to admire the doll. "Akiko hasn't stopped talking about it since yesterday."

Akiko hasn't? Esther thought. *What about Michi?*

"Michi's upstairs. Go on up," Aunt Fumiko said.

Esther climbed up to the room Michi and Akiko shared. The door was closed, and it was quiet. Esther walked in with a smile. "Hi, Michi. What'cha doing?"

Michi was sitting on her bed, reading. Akiko wasn't there. On the dresser was the embroidery hoop. Untouched.

When Michi didn't answer, Esther continued, "Look what I brought."

"Oh."

Silence.

"Wasn't that a fun party?"

"Yeah, until Florence came."

Esther felt squirmy. "I told you, Michi, I *had* to invite her. Mama made me."

"Hmm."

"You don't think I wanted to!"

"How do I know what you wanted?"

Esther gaped at her best friend. How could Michi say such a thing?

"Listen, Michi, you didn't think, you know, what Florence said, about playing together, that I'd ever do that, did you? I'd rather poke out my eyeball with a chopstick than play dolls with Florence!" She grinned, waiting for Michi to laugh.

Michi didn't laugh.

Esther's heart sank. This wasn't going the way it was supposed to. Michi was supposed to get the joke, not glare at her.

"For goodness' sake, Michi, what are you so mad about?"

"As if you don't know."

"I *don't* know. I'm just trying to be nice. Look, I even brought the doll—"

"You don't have to rub it in."

"I'm not rubbing it in! I wanted to share, let you have a turn—"

"So you finally made time for me?"

"What are you talking about?" Esther said. "I came over straight after breakfast."

"After playing with your doll, I bet."

"So? What if I did? Am I not supposed to play with her?" Michi didn't answer.

"Look, Michi, it's not my fault I got the doll and you didn't. So you don't have to be mad at *me*."

"I'm not mad about the stupid doll!" Michi shouted.

Stupid doll!

Michi's face turned red, but she didn't take back her words.

"All right then! If that's the way you want to be, I'll go." Esther took a step toward the door, waiting for Michi to call her back.

Michi said nothing.

Esther ran down the stairs. She slipped out the front door before Aunt Fumiko could say a word.

• • •

Esther stomped down the street. *How can Michi act like that? First turning away from me at the party, then not letting me share, or even explain. And then calling my doll stupid!*

After fuming for a block or two, she began to cool off. *I know Michi didn't mean that Princess Elizabeth was stupid.*

Esther thought for a while. She remembered the hurt look on Michi's face.

Her heart softened. Poor Michi.

How can I fix this? Esther thought.

Her steps slowed. Her mind was blank.

Think, think!

She couldn't think of anything. She couldn't *give* Michi the doll, and it was just rotten luck that only one of them had had her wish come true.

Esther stopped short. *What if Michi's wish could come true too?*

But how? How could Michi get the Princess Margaret doll?

Esther continued walking. Then it came to her. *I'll get it for her! I'll work for it. I'll earn it.*

Esther knew it would be difficult to earn fifteen dollars, and it would take a very long time. Every so often Mama gave her spending money, and she would save that. She swallowed hard, thinking about the jawbreakers she would have to do without. That delicious licorice, that sweet cherry. But she would, for Michi.

And she would ask Mama to give her extra chores and maybe Mama would pay her for them. She would save that money too.

This is exactly what Princess Elizabeth would do, Esther thought, her chest puffing up. *If Princess Elizabeth had a best friend, and if she needed to save up to get something special for her friend, she would make sacrifices to earn the money. Because she's royal. Because it's the right thing to do.*

Esther ran the rest of the way home. Bursting into the kitchen, she said, "Mama! Give me a job. Give me work to do. And will you pay me? I'll do a good job, I promise."

Mama looked up from cutting out butter cookies. She held a doughy hand to Esther's forehead. "Are you feeling all right, sweetheart?"

"Mama! I mean it. I want to save up for something special. So will you give me a job?"

Mama smiled. "Well, I must say, that's very responsible of you, Esther. Hmm, let's see. That windstorm yesterday blew around a bunch of leaves and twigs out front. How about if you rake those up and pile them in the backyard?"

"Sure thing!"

Esther changed into dungarees and grabbed a rake. She surveyed the front yard. Mama wasn't kidding. Leaves and needles were scattered across the front walk and the lawn, along with broken branches and bits of moss.

Esther started raking. Soon she grew warm and unbuttoned her coat. Her arms ached. She leaned on the rake to rest. *Keep going*, she told herself. *It's for Michi.* She gathered everything into a mound, then went to the basement for a metal pail. Scooping armfuls of leaves and twigs, she filled the pail and dumped it beside the garden in the back. It took six trips.

"All done, Mama," Esther said, brushing off her hands.

"Esther, your coat is filthy!" Mama said. "And your hair is full of leaves."

"Never mind my coat, Mama. Come and see." Esther led her to the living room window.

Mama nodded. "You did a very good job. You may take ten cents from my purse."

"Thanks!"

As Esther ran upstairs, she bumped into Grandma Sadie, who was coming down for a cup of tea.

"Estherle!" Grandma Sadie said, removing a leaf from her hair. "What have you been doing?"

"Raking," Esther said. "And look how much I earned." She showed Grandma Sadie the dime.

"You're rich," Grandma Sadie said, winking.

"Say, Grandma Sadie," Esther said as a thought struck, "the next time you're going to buy me something—that is, I'm not saying you *should* buy me something, but in case you are—instead of buying it would you just send me the money? I'm saving up to get a big surprise for someone."

"Sure, Estherle. That's very generous of you. In fact," Grandma Sadie went on, "I'd like to contribute." She slipped a quarter into Esther's hand.

"Thanks, Grandma Sadie!"

She retrieved her piggy bank from the closet and deposited her earnings. Thirty-five whole cents. She had a long way to go, but it was a start. And with Grandma Sadie's help, she'd get there sooner. Just thinking about how happy Michi would be made her smile.

She washed her hands and told Princess Elizabeth the wonderful thing she was planning to do.

CHAPTER 7

The next day, while Esther waited for Michi at their usual corner to walk to school together, she debated when to tell her about the plan.

On one hand, if she told her now, Michi would be really excited. "Esther, that's so nice of you!" she would say, and all the bad feelings from yesterday would melt away.

On the other hand, if she waited until she'd saved the money and actually bought the Princess Margaret doll, it would be such a wonderful surprise. "I worked really hard for this, Michi," she would say, handing over the doll. "It took forever, and I did tons of chores, but it was worth it." Michi would hug the doll and then she would hug Esther.

It'll be more dramatic if I wait, Esther thought, *but I just can't keep the secret for so long!*

"Michi!" Esther said as Michi came to the corner. "I had a brainstorm."

"Did you really," Michi said coldly.

Michi's tone stung. "Yes," Esther said, "but if you don't want to hear it, I won't tell you."

Michi shrugged. "Suit yourself."

Suit yourself? Michi never talked to her like that.

"I will," Esther shot back, even though it was the exact opposite of what she wanted to say.

Noriko and Yoko came along, and Michi stepped forward so that she was standing next to Noriko. Since there was room for only two people side by side on the sidewalk, Esther had to walk with Yoko.

"Did you study for the spelling test, Esther?" Yoko asked.

"Actually, no," Esther said. Between the birthday party and going over to Michi's and raking leaves and taking Grandma Sadie to the train station last night, there hadn't been time. "I think I know the words, though."

"Lucky duck," Yoko said with a sigh. "When I practise them at home, I get them right. But when it comes to the test, I get all mixed up. I forget if it's *I* before *E* in receive, or the other way around, and if exaggerate has one *X* and two *G*s, or two *X*s and one *G*."

"Poor you," Esther said, and she meant it. Yoko was a notoriously bad speller, and nothing seemed to help. But right now Esther wasn't the slightest bit interested in Yoko and the spelling words; she just wanted to switch places with Noriko so she could talk to Michi. But Michi and Noriko had their heads together, and Yoko kept pouring out her troubles, so Esther couldn't make the switch.

At recess Michi joined a group of girls skipping rope. Esther joined in too, but there was never a moment to take Michi aside. The way Michi kept striking up conversations with the other girls and laughing at what they said made Esther think that Michi was avoiding her on purpose.

After school, while Esther changed into her Girl Guides uniform in the girls' washroom, she heard Michi chatting to someone in one of the other stalls. "Akiko begged Mom to let her stay up late so she could see the tea ceremony, and Mom finally said okay, and then Akiko fell asleep and missed the whole thing, and Dad had to carry her home over his shoulder. The next day she was so mad!"

The other girl—Esther could hear that it was Noriko—laughed.

Buttoning up her uniform, Esther fumed. Akiko was *her* special friend, and it should have been Esther, not Noriko, that Michi was telling the story to.

By the time Esther came out and fiddled with her tie, getting it to lie straight, Michi was on her way out of the washroom with Noriko.

Esther stood there, watching the door close behind them. Noriko was as nice as could be, but right now Esther was developing a strong dislike of her. Everyone knew that Esther and Michi walked to Girl Guides together. Everyone. So what business did Noriko have walking with Michi?

Deep down, a small voice said, *It wasn't Noriko's fault. Michi purposely left you behind.*

She pushed the voice away.

To make matters worse, the only person left to walk with to the church where the Guides meetings were held was Florence, who took forever putting on her beret just right and pulling out her golden ringlets to frame her face. By the time they got there, the girls had already formed a circle in the meeting room, and Michi was standing with Noriko on one side of her and Yoko on the other. Esther found a spot on the opposite side of the circle, with Florence beside her. Thankfully Trudy showed up and nudged Esther aside so she could stand next to Florence.

The Guide leaders—Mrs Bingham, Trudy's mother, and Mrs Itani, Yoko's mother—called the meeting to order. All through the singing of "God Save the King" and the recitation of the Girl Guides pledge, Esther tried to catch Michi's eye, but Michi didn't look her way.

The girls sat on the floor. Mrs Bingham fetched a cardboard box and placed it in the centre of the circle. "Now then, girls, before we start our craft, let's collect our metal. What do you all have today?"

Esther's stomach plummeted. Each week, as a contribution to the war effort, the girls brought in discarded metal items. The metal was melted down and reused. At each meeting, the girl who brought the most metal won a small prize.

Esther had nothing today. In the excitement and upset of the weekend, she had forgotten all about it.

One by one the girls came forward and placed their items in the box. Doris brought a couple of flattened tin cans. Ella, whose mother was a hairdresser in a beauty salon, put in a handful of bent bobby pins. Florence stood

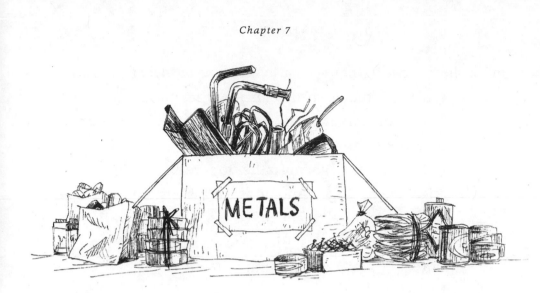

up and with a great flourish handed over a tall can that
had held tennis balls.

"Excellent, Florence!" Mrs Bingham said.

Florence beamed.

Mrs Itani turned to Esther. "Esther?"

"I don't have anything today. Sorry. I just... don't."

Mrs Bingham clicked her tongue. "As Girl Guides, we
have to set a good example and do our part."

Esther's face burned. She looked down.

"I'm sure you'll remember next time, Esther," Mrs Itani
said kindly.

Esther nodded, not trusting herself to speak.

They continued around the circle. When it was Michi's
turn, she took a paper bag from behind her back. Grinning,

she removed what at first looked like an oversized silver grapefruit. Esther gasped, realizing what it was.

"Michiko!" Mrs Itani said. "Is that entire ball made of aluminium strips?"

Michi nodded. "I got my father to save all the strips from his cigarette packages. And he asked his customers to save theirs too. I collected them all."

"My goodness," Mrs Bingham said, "there must be hundreds of pieces of aluminium in there!"

Michi beamed.

"You certainly win the prize this week, Michiko," Mrs Itani said, and handed over a pink eraser.

Michi held out the eraser to show Noriko and Yoko. Esther watched as they patted her best friend on the back. Words came out of her mouth before she could stop them. "That's not fair. Michi gets extra help because of her daddy's store."

"Maybe I just try harder," Michi shot back. "Maybe you forgot because you had other things you cared about more."

Esther stared at her. Michi had never spoken to her like this. And in front of everybody. She felt her cheeks flame.

"Now girls, it doesn't matter where the metal comes from, because it all goes to a good cause, doesn't it?" Mrs Bingham said. "Come gather around the table. For our craft today, we're going to make sock puppets to donate to children. Choose two buttons for the eyes and one for the nose..."

Esther didn't hear any more. Her ears were ringing; she didn't know if it was her blood pounding or Michi's words or the chatter of the girls as they took their places around the table. She didn't even bother to try to sit next to Michi. Without looking, she knew that Michi would be flanked by Noriko and Yoko. Esther drifted to the table and found herself next to Florence, who was combing through a bowl of buttons, trying to find the two prettiest ones.

Esther chose two buttons at random. She threaded her needle with embroidery thread and started sewing the first one on.

Florence tittered. "Your buttons don't match, Esther. Your puppet's eyes will be cockeyed."

Trudy tittered too.

Esther looked. One button was green and the other was brown. She shrugged. "Who cares?" She continued sewing and felt a sharp prick. She pulled her hand out from inside the sock. A bright drop of blood splashed onto the table.

"Eewww!" Florence squealed. "Don't bleed on my puppet!"

Esther looked at her finger. A bead of blood hovered on the tip. She stuck her finger in her mouth.

Mrs Bingham hurried over in response to Florence's cries of "Esther's bleeding!"

At the other end of the table, Michi giggled as she sewed on her puppet's nose. Perfectly, of course.

CHAPTER 8

*T*hat night at dinner, Esther wasn't very hungry. Mama had made sloppy joes, her favourite. But Esther ate only a few mouthfuls and put down her bun.

Mama held the back of her hand to Esther's forehead. "No fever," she said, looking at her quizzically. She smiled. "Too much birthday excitement, I suppose."

"I'll eat hers," Jake said, reaching across the table.

Mama rolled her eyes. "Jake Shulman, I swear you have a hollow leg."

Jake grinned. "Hockey practice today." He went on excitedly, "And guess what. We're going to play a scrimmage between periods at a Vancouver Lions game at the end of the season!"

"Why, Jake, that's terrific," Daddy said.

"Tomo and I have been practising our secret play."

"Your secret play?"

"Yeah." Jake jumped up and put his fists together, one above the other. "Tomo passes to me. I fake a shot but flip

it to my backhand." Jake twisted his wrists back and forth as if moving his hockey stick. "Then I pass to him, skate up ice, he passes, quick shot—" Jake mimed a slap shot. "He shoots, he scores!" he shouted, doing his best Foster Hewitt impression.

Mama and Daddy laughed as Jake raised his fist in the air. Esther was glad they were distracted.

• • •

That night it was Esther's turn to wash and Jake's turn to dry. While Esther filled the washing-up basin with soapy water, Mama poured herself and Daddy cups of coffee.

"So, how was your day, Herbie?" Mama asked. "Anything new at the paper?" Daddy was the editor of the *Vancouver Messenger*.

Daddy tipped his head. He and Mama carried their cups into the living room. As Esther slid the dirty dishes into the soapy water, Jake said, "Maybe we'll get all the Lions' autographs. Wouldn't that be swell?"

Esther thought of the autograph book Michi had given her, the words that Michi had written: "You're the friend I love the best."

Some best friend, Esther thought. She scrubbed a plate furiously, splashing water.

"...able to get any information about Anna and Josef?" she heard Mama say.

Just as Daddy started to answer, Jake took the rinsed dish from her and started drying it. "I'll have to make sure my skates are sharpened just right. They're old and they don't hold an edge so well anymore—" He stopped when Esther poked him. "What? I'm drying the dishes as fast as you hand them to me."

She put her finger to her lips and cocked her head toward the living room. Jake caught Esther's eye. He nodded.

"No. I contacted the International Red Cross..."

Esther silently swished the sponge over a dish. Jake quietly placed a clean pan on the stove.

" . . . but they didn't have any information about their whereabouts."

"Oh, dear. Another dead end."

"The person I spoke to said it was almost impossible to keep track of people, the way they're fleeing from country to country."

"Especially if they're in hiding," Mama said.

"That's not all," Daddy went on. "Today we got a wire saying that the Nazis were rounding up Jews and sending them to transit camps in Germany and Poland."

"What's a transit camp?" Mama asked.

Rinsing a plate, Esther held her breath.

"It's a place where people are held before they're sent to a work camp."

"How awful! I hope they managed to escape Germany," Mama said.

"Even so, they may not be safe. Apparently they are capturing Jews in the occupied countries, too, like Holland and France."

"Oh my God," Mama said.

"I'll try to get some more information about the camps," Daddy said.

Mama sighed. "I wish this war would end."

Esther swished the wash water as quietly as she could, and Jake put away the dried dishes with the utmost care.

"It's awfully quiet in there," Mama called. "What are you two up to?"

"Hey, we're not fighting for once, so don't complain," Jake called back.

Esther shot him a smile.

• • •

Up in her room, Esther's heart lifted when she saw the Princess Elizabeth doll lying on her pillow. She lifted the doll and Elizabeth's eyes blinked open. Esther smiled at her.

Then she remembered the awful things Michi had said.

You don't have to rub it in.

The stupid doll.

Suit yourself.

And then the worst: *Maybe I just try harder. Maybe you forgot because you had other things you cared about more.*

Esther jumped up. She emptied her piggy bank. The thirty-five cents fell into her hand. If Michi was going to be so mean, insulting her, and not letting her explain the plan, and chumming around with other girls, and ignoring her, her best friend, then there was no point in saving up to buy her the Princess Margaret doll.

"Just think of all the jawbreakers I'll be able to buy," Esther said out loud. "All the licorice and lemon and cherry I like."

Defiantly, she put on her cape and held the Princess Elizabeth doll out in front of her. She waved Elizabeth's arms up and down. She strolled around her room, moving Elizabeth's legs left, right, left, right. She tossed her head and said, "Aren't the roses dee-vine this year, Margaret?"

"Yes, they are, and their scent is mah-velous, Elizabeth."

Esther felt silly talking to herself. She put Princess Elizabeth's arms straight out in front of her and galloped around the room, bouncing Elizabeth up and down in the saddle just like she had with Michi.

Esther stopped.

This was no fun.

She took off her cape and put Princess Elizabeth back on the pillow. The doll's eyes shut with a faint click.

CHAPTER 9

A few days later, Esther, Jake and Mama strolled down Cordova Street, Esther and Jake each swinging a bag labelled Adachi's Shoes. Jake had just got a new pair of runners; Esther, new saddle shoes.

They ambled along, enjoying rare February sunshine. They turned down Hastings Street and passed Rafelson's Toy Shop. Esther's heart leaped to see Princess Margaret still in the window.

Then it fell.

So much for my wonderful plan.

Suddenly Mama said, "Let's drop in on Daddy, what do you say?"

"Yes!" Esther and Jake cheered.

They didn't often visit Daddy at work, and Esther loved it when they did. She loved riding up to the fifth floor in the elevator, with its shiny brass grille that slowly slid open and closed. She loved spinning around in Daddy's office chair until she got dizzy.

When they entered the *Vancouver Messenger* offices, Miss Bakstrom, the receptionist, looked startled to see them. "Oh—uh—good afternoon, Mrs Shulman."

Mama didn't seem to notice. "Good afternoon, Miss Bakstrom. Is my husband in?"

"Yes, but … uh … I believe he's busy at the moment."

Esther heard raised voices. They were coming from down the hall. *Is one of those voices Daddy's?*

A door opened, then slammed. A man strode down the hall toward them. Esther recognized him. He was Mr O'Toole, Daddy's boss. She and Jake always laughed about the way he wore his thin brown hair parted way over on the side to cover up his bald spot.

No one was laughing today. Mr O'Toole marched through reception. He glanced their way, missed half a step, then continued on, without a word, into the men's room.

A moment later, the same office door opened. Daddy came out, crossed the hall to his own office, and slammed the door behind him. Immediately, he opened it, turning back in surprise.

"Gladdy? What are you doing here?"

"We thought we'd surprise you. But if this isn't a good time..."

"No, it's fine. Come in."

Bewildered, Esther, Jake and Mama filed into Daddy's office. He closed the door, gently this time. His hair was dishevelled. His face was red.

"Herbie, what's the matter?"

Daddy looked at Esther and Jake, then at Mama. "I don't think I should talk about it right now."

"Come on, Daddy," Jake said. "We know something is wrong."

Daddy opened that day's newspaper and held it up. "Mr O'Toole was upset with my editorial."

Esther read: NEW RESTRICTIONS ON JAPANESE ARE UNJUST.

"What new restrictions?" Mama asked.

"Enemy alien cards. All Japanese Canadians have to register as 'enemy aliens.' Even if they were born here."

"What!"

"Even kids?" Esther said.

"Even kids."

Poor Michi, Esther thought. Even though she didn't understand exactly what "enemy alien" meant, she knew right away it was something bad.

Daddy went on, "My editorial says that those measures are a violation of their rights as Canadian citizens. O'Toole wasn't pleased. He said it's not appropriate to question government policy. He accused me of being unpatriotic."

"That's ridiculous!" Mama said. She pointed to the headline. "And you're right. Those restrictions are unjust."

"That's exactly what I said. Only not so politely."

"Even so, I don't know if it's a good idea to get your boss mad at you, Herbie. After all, you could lose your job."

"I'm surprised at you, Gladdy. I know you agree with me."

Mama blushed. "Of course I do. But O'Toole looked furious."

"O'Toole wouldn't stand up to the government if his life depended on it," Daddy snapped.

"Yes, but…" Her voice trailed off. Then she took a breath. "No. I'm being silly. You're right. You keep doing what you're doing."

Daddy looked surprised. He hugged Mama. They spoke a little longer, and then the three of them left.

• • •

The next day, when Michi came to the corner, Esther swallowed hard. For the past several mornings, they'd barely said hello to each other. But today Esther felt she had to say something. "Listen, Michi, I heard bad things are happening, and I just want you to know—"

Michi turned away. "It's not your problem, Esther."

"What! How can you say that? You know I—"

Before she could finish, Noriko and Yoko came. Michi walked with Yoko. Esther saw Yoko's shoulders shaking, and heard quiet sobs. Michi put her arm around her. Noriko stepped forward and took Yoko's hand.

Esther watched the three girls walk on, leaving her behind.

It's not fair of Michi to block me out like this, Esther thought.

The two of them had never made an issue of being Japanese or white or Christian or Jewish. They were just Esther and Michi. Best friends.

Or at least we used to be.

CHAPTER 10

"Jake, come here!"

It was a week later, and Esther stood at the living room window. Men, about a dozen of them, were walking down the street, all heading in the same direction. It was a blustery day, and they were wearing topcoats and hats. Most were carrying suitcases or duffle bags. Some had bundles tucked under their arms.

Why are they marching down the street? Esther thought.

After a moment, she realized that they were all Japanese men. She recognized the fathers, uncles and brothers of her friends. There was Mr Adachi, Noriko's father. There was Mr Itani, Yoko's father, and Hiro, Yoko's older brother, and, behind them were Yoko and her mother and her little brother, Jun. Esther thought she saw tears rolling down Yoko's face, steaming up her glasses.

Jake pushed in beside Esther. He gaped.

"What's going on?" Esther asked.

"Let's find out."

Jake dashed down the steps, Esther at his heels. When

they got down to the street, more men had joined the throng. They marched, eyes straight ahead, hands gripping the handles of their valises. There was the murmur of voices, the occasional muffled sob.

Some neighbours stood on their doorsteps. A few waved goodbye.

Next door, Mr Harper yelled from his doorstep, "Good riddance!"

"See? I told you Mr Harper must've put up that cartoon," Esther told Jake.

She felt like yelling, *Shut up!* but she didn't. Mama would have a fit if she heard her speak like that to a grown-up.

Hiro Itani took a step toward Mr Harper. His mother pulled him back, speaking in a low but urgent voice. His face dark red, Hiro walked on.

"Look! There's Uncle Ted," Jake said, pointing.

Halfway down the block, the Suzukis were huddled together. A suitcase sat at Uncle Ted's feet. He was carrying Akiko, her arms wrapped around his neck. Aunt Fumiko stood beside him. Tomo's arms were folded across his chest. Michi stood as straight as a pin, the wind blowing her black hair across her face.

Esther and Jake took off. As she ran, Esther thought, *Will Michi speak to me?* But right now it didn't matter. There was trouble, and she had to go to her friend.

When Esther and Jake reached the Suzukis, Jake asked, "What's happening?"

Aunt Fumiko turned. "Oh, Jake . . . Esther . . . " Her eyes were red.

Michi glanced over. Her eyes were red too. She took a step closer to her dad.

"They're sending us away," Uncle Ted said.

"What? Who's sending who away?" Esther asked.

"The government. Sending away all Japanese men and boys over eighteen."

"But . . ." Esther was so confused she couldn't think straight. "Why?"

"Because we're at war with Japan. They think we won't be loyal. They say we might give secrets to the Japanese."

"That's crazy!" she said.

"We know that!" Tomo exploded. "It's ridiculous. We're loyal Canadians."

"Where are they sending you?" Jake asked.

"To work camps, somewhere in the Interior. We're going to build roads."

Roads! Esther thought. *Uncle Ted's a shopkeeper. How's he supposed to build roads?*

They all stood there, too miserable to speak. Finally, Uncle Ted said, "I should go."

"Daddy!" Akiko cried, holding him tighter.

"Michi . . ." Esther said, holding out her hand.

Michi didn't turn. Her shoulders stiffened.

Jake nudged Esther. "Come on, Es. Let's leave them alone."

Esther followed. Behind her, she could hear Uncle Ted's low voice, Aunt Fumiko's quiet weeping. And other crying that she was sure was Michi's. Crying that she could do nothing about.

• • •

The next night at dinner, Mama said to Daddy, "What did Mr O'Toole think about today's editorial?"

The newspaper was on the coffee table. The headline read: JAPANESE MEN EXILED: FOR SHAME.

Daddy didn't answer.

"Everybody was talking about it at school today," Jake said. "Half the kids' dads have already been sent away, and the rest will be going soon. Everybody's upset."

Daddy exchanged a look with Mama, then nodded. "O'Toole's even unhappier than he was before. He's putting pressure on me to tone it down." He ran a hand through his hair. "I've been thinking. Maybe you're right, Gladdy. Maybe I should toe the line."

"No!"

Esther was surprised to hear Mama say that, especially since she had said the exact opposite the other day.

Daddy must have been surprised too, because his eyes opened wide. "No? But I thought you—"

"Yes. I did. I was afraid. But this is so outrageous, so awful, it's beyond anything. Someone has to speak out."

"You do realize I might get fired?"

Mama laughed nervously. "I'd just as soon you kept your job, Herbie. But you can't keep quiet about this."

Daddy leaned over and kissed her cheek. "I knew I could count on you, Gladdy."

Esther squeezed Daddy's hand. Her brave father, standing up to the government, telling them they were wrong.

Then a sudden fear struck her. She pictured the Japanese men walking down the street, the faces of the women and children left behind. She burst into tears.

"Esther! What is it, sweetheart?" Daddy said.

"They won't send you away, will they?" she said through her tears.

"Don't worry about that." He rubbed the tears from her cheeks. "Okay now?"

Esther nodded. *As long as what happened to Michi doesn't happen to me.*

She felt terrible as soon as she thought it. But that was how she felt.

CHAPTER 11

*O*ne day after school, about a week later, without really realizing where she was going, Esther found herself at Suzuki's Store. When she opened the door, she was surprised to see that it was nearly empty.

That's odd, she thought.

It hadn't exactly been bustling a few weeks ago, when she and the others had stopped in after the movie, but it hadn't been this dead. Then she recalled Mama saying that, with the men gone, a lot of Japanese families were struggling to make ends meet. Maybe that was why so few people were shopping.

Aunt Fumiko was at the cash register. Akiko sat on a stool at her side, drumming her feet against its legs like a woodpecker tapping on a tree. Aunt Fumiko looked tired. There were circles under her eyes, and her black hair was messy, as if she had been running her hands through it.

Akiko tugged at her mother's sleeve. "Mommy? Can you play with me now?"

Aunt Fumiko shook her head as a customer came up to the till. "Not now, honey. Maybe later." She took the customer's

money and managed a weak smile as she handed back the change. "Thank you, come again."

"Now, Mommy?" Akiko said.

"Sorry, Kiko. Not till after work—oh, hi, Esther." A smile lit up her face. "What brings you in?"

"Nothing, really," Esther said, and in fact she didn't know why she had come. Mama hadn't asked her to pick anything up. She didn't have money for a jawbreaker. "Just wanted to say hi."

Aunt Fumiko peered at her. "Are you okay, Esther? We haven't seen much of you lately."

So Michi hasn't told her, Esther thought. "Fine, fine," she said. "Just busy."

Akiko ran out from behind the cash register and hugged her. "Esther! I'm so bored my legs are jiggly."

Aunt Fumiko looked embarrassed. "Not much fun for her here."

"I could take her to the playground."

"Yes, please!" Akiko shouted.

"Would you, Esther? Just for a little while. Tomo is delivering papers, and Michi is working on a Girl Guide badge—well, I guess you know all about that—"

The Guides were collecting tree leaves for a badge in woodland lore. *Michi must be doing it with someone else.*

"—so poor Kiko is stuck with me."

"I'd love to," Esther said, and, taking Akiko's hand, led her out of the store. As they walked down the street toward the school playground, Akiko said, "Guess what, Esther. I can print my name now."

"You can? Your whole name?"

"Yup. *A – K – I – K - O.*"

"Wow. Did you learn that in kindergarten?"

"Yup. And I can even print Suzuki. It has two *Us*." Akiko held up two fingers.

"That's right. It does."

"But sometimes I get the letters mixed up."

"That's okay. You'll get it straight," Esther told her.

They went on the see-saw, the swings and the merry-go-round. When Akiko stopped asking for "just one more spin, pretty please?" Esther figured she must be tired, and

they headed back to Suzuki's Store. As they were leaving the playground, Esther heard voices. She glanced across the street.

Michi was walking with Yoko and Noriko. Their hands were full of leaves.

"Look, Esther!" Akiko said. "Michi, Michi! Esther took me to the playground!" She tugged Esther toward the opposite sidewalk.

Esther had hoped that she and Akiko wouldn't be noticed, but it was too late. As she crossed the street with Akiko, she saw Michi glance at her, then look away.

"Hi, Esther," Noriko and Yoko said, and Esther greeted them back.

There was a silence. "Guess what, Michi," Akiko said, skipping beside her sister. "Esther held me up on the see-saw, way up high, and she wouldn't let me down for the longest time. It was fun!"

"That's nice," Michi said in a flat voice.

Another silence. "I guess you can take Akiko back," Esther said, not looking at Michi. "Tell Aunt Fumiko I said 'bye."

She turned down her street. Akiko's voice, excitedly telling Michi, Noriko and Yoko all about her adventure, followed Esther home.

CHAPTER 12

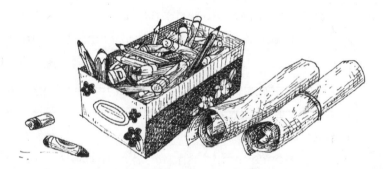

A few days later, Esther sat at the kitchen table, doing her homework. Mama and Daddy were in the living room, talking softly. Jake was at hockey practice. It was after dinner, but now, in March, the days were longer, and a shaft of light from the setting sun slanted across the table, creating a pool of golden light.

Esther opened her spelling book, placed it right in the pool and started copying her words.

Cooperate.

What sentence could she make up with the word cooperate? She thought for a minute. *All the students in the class must cooperate.*

Forlorn.

A sentence sprang into her mind: *Michi looked forlorn when her father was sent away.*

She couldn't write that. But it was true. Michi had looked devastated. All the Japanese kids at school had. Yoko had even cried a few times, her cheeks red with embarrassment, and Miss McTavish had sent Noriko to the washroom with her.

Forlorn. Forlorn.

The little boy was forlorn when his balloon floated away, she wrote.

Betray—

The telephone rang. Esther jumped up. "Esther Shulman speaking."

"Estherle! How are you, *mommie-shainie*?"

"Grandma Sadie, how are you?"

"I'm all right." She didn't sound all right. She sounded worried, like she had when she was in Vancouver. "How is your savings campaign going?"

"My what? Oh—it's over. I stopped it."

"Really? I thought you were saving to buy something for somebody."

"Yeah, I was, but . . . never mind. You don't have to send me any more money."

"Hmm. So, how is Princess Elizabeth?" Grandma Sadie said.

"Oh, she's . . . uh . . . wonderful, Grandma. I play with her all the time."

There was a pause. "You all right, Estherle? You sound funny."

"I'm fine."

"Hmm. Listen, can I talk to your daddy?"

"Sure, I'll go get him."

Daddy, who must have heard Esther greet Grandma Sadie, was already standing in the doorway. Esther handed him the telephone.

"Hi, Mama, how are you?"

Esther headed back to the kitchen table, but Mama called from the living room. "Esther, come in here with me."

"I'm doing my homework."

"He's sure it was her?" Daddy said into the telephone.

"*Esther.*"

"Oh, all right."

She plopped down next to Mama on the couch.

Esther asked, "Is it about Aunt Anna?"

Mama hesitated. "Probably."

Esther's stomach clenched.

"It could be good," Mama said, but she didn't sound convinced.

After a few minutes, Daddy said, "Goodnight, Mama. Try not to worry." He hung up and came into the living room.

"Well?" Mama said.

Daddy looked at her, then at Esther. "Esther, sweetheart, I don't think—"

"I know what it's about, Daddy."

Her parents traded looks. Daddy sat down. "Grandma Sadie heard from an old neighbour in Berlin that Aunt Anna and Uncle Josef were heading to the Swiss border. A friend of Anna's lives there, and he said he would try to help them cross the border into Switzerland."

"That would be wonderful," Mama said.

"So they would be safe in Switzerland?" Esther asked.

"Probably. If they make it." Daddy passed a hand over his eyes. "If they're caught they will be sent to a work camp."

"Is that like where Uncle Ted is?" Esther asked.

"Worse."

"Herbie—"

"Michi must be pretty upset about her dad, eh?"

Esther felt her cheeks grow warm. "Yeah, I guess so. I mean, yeah, she is."

"I can't bear it," Mama said. "Fumiko's run off her feet, what with trying to manage the store and take care of the family." She looked at her watch. "You know what? It's not that late. I've got a whole extra pan of brisket left over from tonight. I'll take it over right now." She stood up. "Want to go with me, Esther?"

Esther looked down. "I've got to finish my homework."

Daddy held his hand against Esther's forehead. "Are you sick? That's the first time I've ever heard you use homework as an excuse not to see Michi."

Giving a weak smile, Esther went back in the kitchen.

Betray.

She picked up her pencil.

The two girls were best friends until one betrayed the other, she wrote.

But who betrayed whom?

• • •

That night, Mama came to tuck Esther in. "Poor Aunt Fumiko," she said, smoothing a curl away from Esther's forehead. "She's exhausted. Tomo's been delivering papers, and Michi's been doing the cooking. But I guess you know all that already."

"Mmmm," Esther said.

Mama gave her a sharp look. "Are things okay with you and Michi? She hasn't been around much."

Esther's hands tightened on her blanket. For a moment she was tempted to tell Mama everything—Michi getting mad at her at the party, her failed plan to get Michi the Princess Margaret doll, Michi's snub at Girl Guides and Michi playing with Noriko and Yoko, instead of with her. She felt a lump in her throat, like a cork in a bottle. If she could just push that lump out...

But no. She didn't want to admit that she and her best friend had hurt each other. She didn't know if she even had a best friend.

"We're okay, Mama. Michi's just been busy lately."

Mama looked like she didn't believe her, but she leaned over and kissed Esther's cheek. Then she tenderly traced a finger down the arm of Princess Elizabeth, who was lying next to Esther on the pillow.

"Still thrilled with your birthday present, I see."

"Yeah."

Mama grinned. "Did you know it was Jake who told Grandma Sadie about the doll?"

"Jake?"

Mama nodded. "Not so awful, your big brother, eh? I told Grandma Sadie it was too extravagant. But she said,

'If I want to spoil my granddaughter, I will.' And then, the look on your face when you saw the doll—pure joy!"

CHAPTER 13

You are invited, the card said in fancy letters. At recess, Florence marched across the playground, handing out birthday invitations to selected girls like a queen bestowing favours on her subjects.

Do I have to? was Esther's first thought, but she knew the answer was yes. Florence had invited her last year, so she'd had to invite Florence this year, and now Florence was inviting her again. It was an endless trap.

• • •

On the day of the party, Esther put on her Rosh Hashanah dress, tied her hair in two curly pigtails and grabbed her present, a Nancy Drew book.

Florence answered the door wearing a tiara. Its shiny silver metal reflected the light, and four rubies formed a diamond shape on the front. It balanced on top of her perfect golden ringlets.

What's going on? Esther thought. Then, as she came inside, she saw that all the other girls—Trudy, Ella, Doris

and a few others from their class—were wearing tiaras too. Only theirs were homemade, cardboard covered with silver paper, and without the glittering gems.

Ella and Doris giggled at each other, standing in front of a hallway mirror. "You look funny, Dolittle."

It was true, Esther thought. Doris had thick blonde pigtails, and the tiara, perched on the very top of her head, looked like it was going to pop off at any moment.

Doris elbowed her friend. "*You* should talk, Elephant."

Ella chortled. Her tiara was slipping down her thin face, falling over her forehead.

Florence stuck a tiara on Esther's head. "Welcome to my court, Lady Esther."

That was when Esther got it. Florence was the queen and the rest of them were her courtiers. *How ridiculous,* she thought.

"Come in, my ladies," Florence said, leading the girls into the living room. "We have to choose my princess."

"Isn't that what we are?" Ella said.

Florence shook her head. "You're ladies-in-waiting. There's only one princess."

"Me, me!" Trudy said, waving her hand in the air.

Florence giggled. "To make it fair, we're going to play pass the parcel."

She instructed the girls to sit in a circle. Florence's mother handed her a package wrapped in shiny paper, then put on a record. The strains of *Cow-Cow Boogie* rang out. Florence passed the parcel to Trudy, and it made its way around the circle.

"Oh, please me," Trudy breathed.

Oh, please not me, Esther thought.

"Come a ti-yi,-yeah, Come a ti-yippity-yi-yeah," sang the record. The parcel came around a second time. Just as Esther was about to hand it to Trudy, the music stopped. Trudy's hand was touching the package, but it was still firmly in Esther's grip.

Oh, no, Esther thought.

"It's Esther!" Florence said.

"And I was so close." Trudy was on the verge of tears.

"You know what, Trudy?" Esther said. "You can have it. You were practically there."

"Can I really?" Trudy said, her face lighting up.

"That's nice of you, Esther," Doris said.

Esther gave a modest smile.

"Open it, open it," Florence said. Trudy tore off the wrapping. Inside lay a silver tiara, not as large as Florence's but larger than the other girls', with three small blue stones glued on the front. Trudy flung off her cardboard tiara and carefully placed the silver one on her head. Her bright red hair curled out beneath it.

"Now you're Princess Trudy," Florence said.

"Oh, I'm so excited!" Trudy said. "What do I do?"

"Wait on me, fetch me things, be in charge of the ladies-in-waiting."

"Yes, Your Majesty!"

After birthday cake, it was time for presents. Once again the girls sat in a circle in the living room. Each girl presented her gift to Princess Trudy, who delivered it, with a curtsey, to Queen Florence.

Florence was gracious, Esther had to admit. Whatever the present—note cards, lacy socks, crayons, nail polish— she politely thanked the girl who had given it and said she loved it and that it was just what she wanted. When she opened Esther's gift, she said, "Oh, *The Clue of the Tapping Heels*. I don't have this one. Thanks."

"I haven't read it yet myself," Esther said, hoping Florence would offer to loan it to her when she was finished with it.

Florence's mother handed Trudy one more gift to deliver to Florence. "This is from Daddy and me," she said.

It was a large box, wrapped in Rafelson's paper. Florence carefully peeled back the tape, as she had done with all the other gifts, unfolding the paper and smoothing it out before opening the box.

"Oh!" For the first time, Florence sounded truly surprised. "I was hoping—oh, Mommy!"

She jumped up and gave her mother a hug. Then she held the box out facing the girls.

It was the Princess Margaret doll. She looked exactly as Esther remembered her from Rafelson's window. The navy, green and red plaid skirt. The ruffled white blouse.

The maroon cardigan. The glittering black Mary Janes. The rosy cheeks. The curled dark-brown hair.

"Look, everybody!"

"Oh, you lucky duck," Trudy said.

"Isn't she just beautiful?" Florence said, taking the doll out of the box.

"Can we see?" Ella said as she and the other girls crowded closer.

Florence showed them the tiny fastenings of the shoes, the pearl buttons on the blouse. The girls squealed and exclaimed.

Esther sat there in disbelief. In dismay. Even though her plan to get the doll for Michi had fizzled, she hadn't given up hope that somehow it would work out, and she had held on to the thirty-five cents. She hadn't bought a single jawbreaker. But now the plan was completely crushed.

"Esther!" Florence called over the heads of the other girls. "We can play princesses together!"

·❀·· · ·❀·· · ·❀·

CHAPTER 14

*O*n Monday, Florence carried her Princess Margaret doll out to the playground. All the girls ran over and squealed, "Oh, Florence, you lucky thing!" "Oh, Florence, how beautiful!" Noriko and Yoko went over and carefully touched the pressed pleats of Princess Margaret's skirt, the soft wool of her sweater.

Michi stayed on the outside of the circle, studiously not looking Florence's way, but when she caught sight of the doll in Florence's arms, she stopped dead. Her mouth fell open.

Esther couldn't stand it. She hurried over. In a low voice, she said, "I didn't want her to get it, Michi."

"Really?"

"Yes, really!"

Michi didn't answer.

Desperately Esther blurted, "Want to come over after school?"

"No, thank you."

Noriko and Yoko came back, sighing over how beautiful

the Princess Margaret doll was, and Michi turned to them.
The three girls started playing hopscotch.

Esther wasn't invited to join in. She stomped away,
then stood on the playground, alone, eating her snack, an
oatmeal cookie that Mama had made. Carefully chewing
around the raisins, saving them for last, she looked for
someone to play with.

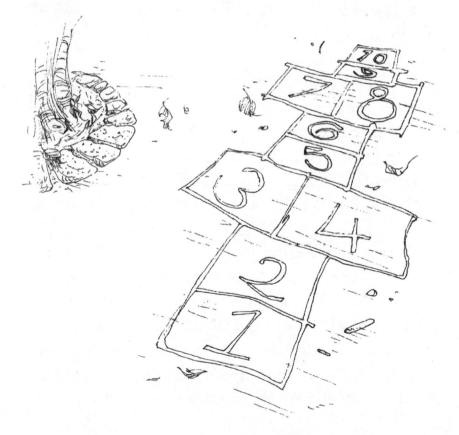

Doris ran by, chasing a red-and-white beach ball. Esther turned. Ella had thrown the ball, and Esther watched as a gust of wind blew it a few steps out of Doris' reach, and then, just as Doris caught up to it, blew it away again.

"Come here, you silly ball," Doris huffed. She was on the chubby side and not as good an athlete as Ella.

Ella laughed. "I don't think talking to the ball will help, Dolittle."

Esther knew that Ella and Doris were usually a twosome, but she didn't think they'd mind letting someone else join. She took a step forward.

Just then, Florence, the doll cradled in her arms, marched up to Esther. Trudy trailed behind her, pretending to carry the train of her robe, chanting, "Yes, Your Highness. No, Your Highness. Very good, Your Highness."

Florence called, "Esther, want to come over after school with your Princess Elizabeth doll? We can play princesses together."

Not on your life, Esther nearly blurted. Then she glanced at Michi. Something about the stiff set of Michi's shoulders, as she prepared to throw her hopscotch rock, told Esther that Michi had heard. But Michi didn't turn around, didn't look at Esther. She didn't say, "Don't go." She didn't say, "Come to my house instead." She threw her rock onto the seven square and started jumping, one-two, three, four-five, six, sailing over the big rectangle of seven as if she hadn't a care in the world.

Well, if that's the way you want to be.

"Sure, Florence," Esther said loudly. "That sounds like fun. I'll get my doll and come right after school."

. . .

"Put your doll here, Esther." Florence pointed to the window seat in her bedroom. A three-sided bay window overlooked the garden. In front of the window was a wooden bench covered with a floral cushion. Esther bent Princess Elizabeth's legs so she could sit, and placed her next to Princess Margaret on the cushion. The two dolls looked lovely side by side.

She had never been in Florence's room before. It was twice the size of hers. The bed was covered with a ruffled pink bedspread, and there were so many stuffed animals on it that Esther couldn't imagine how Florence got into bed at night. Paintings of fairies covered the walls, and on a shelf sat half a dozen old-fashioned, porcelain-faced dolls in long skirts and ruffled blouses. They looked like they'd never been played with. In the corner stood an enormous dollhouse, nearly as big as Esther's dresser at home.

When Florence said her dollhouse was like a palace, she wasn't kidding, Esther thought.

"Shall we have tea, Elizabeth?" Florence said.

Esther smiled. "Oh, yes, do let's."

Florence went over to the dollhouse and took out a miniature tea set: teapot, cups, saucers, even a sugar bowl and milk pitcher, all in fine white china with a pattern of violets on it. She set them next to the two dolls and pretended to pour. "Here you go, Elizabeth."

"Thank you, Margaret."

Esther raised the cup to Elizabeth's mouth. "Why, this tea is delicious."

"Hold your saucer right underneath the cup," Florence said. "That's the only proper way to drink tea."

"Oh, sorry." Esther held the cup in one hand and the saucer directly beneath it in the other.

"Do have a cucumber sandwich," Florence said, handing out a tiny plate. "But don't drop any crumbs!"

Pretending to eat, Esther thought what they could do next. Something a *little* more fun. "Shall we explore Buckingham Palace, Margaret?"

"Certainly. Just let me put the tea things away." Carefully, Florence put every piece of china back in the dollhouse. She lifted Princess Margaret and straightened her legs. Esther did the same with Princess Elizabeth. Working the dolls' legs, they slowly promenaded them along the edge of the window seat.

"Shall we slide down the banisters, Margaret?" Esther said.

Florence shook her head. "Oh, no, that wouldn't be ladylike." She continued walking Princess Margaret at a decorous pace.

Esther kept the rhythm. Down to one end of the window seat, turn around, and back again. Step, step, step. "Let's go outside and have a frolic in the garden, shall we?"

"Oh, yes, lovely idea." Florence held her doll up so it could see out the window.

"Aren't we really going outside?" Esther asked.

"Oh, no! We might get dirty," Florence answered. She sat Princess Margaret back down on the window seat, raised the doll's arms and pushed her hands together. "Let's knit blankets for the brave soldiers."

Esther sighed. She moved Elizabeth's hands to knit. After several minutes, she picked up her doll. "Florence, I have to go. Thank you for having me."

"So soon? Well, goodbye." She waved Margaret's arm. "Come back tomorrow. We'll go to Westminster Abbey and say prayers for the troops."

Esther hid a yawn.

Walking home, she thought, *Say prayers for the troops?* If it had been Michi, they would have run the princesses around and danced them and had them eat too many crumpets and—heaven forbid—made them do unladylike things, like spill their tea or step in dog poop.

But it wasn't Michi. And now that Florence had the Princess Margaret doll, it wasn't ever going to be Michi.

CHAPTER 15

A few days later, Esther was in her room when the telephone rang.

Mama answered. "Herbie! It's not like you to call during the day. Is something wrong?" Silence. "They're *what?... Everyone?... Where?*"

What are Mama and Daddy talking about?

"Why, that's awful!" Mama said. She listened some more. "Thanks for telling me, Herbie. Yes, I'll go right away." She put the phone down. "Jake! Esther! Come down here."

When Esther and Jake came into the living room, Mama was tying on her kerchief. There were tears in her eyes.

"Mama, what is it?" Jake asked.

"Oh, that bloody government," Mama said, wiping her eyes. "They're sending the Japanese away."

"Who—what do you mean?" Esther said.

"Daddy just called. He saw a memo. They're moving all the Japanese away from the West Coast."

"You mean the families?" Jake asked.

Mama nodded, grabbing her purse. "*Everybody.* Women, children, old people. Oh, of all the unjust, boneheaded moves."

"Tomo—going away?" Jake said just as Esther blurted, "Michi—going away?"

Mama nodded. "Come on. I've got to go to Fumiko. Let's see if there is anything we can do."

Esther's stomach clenched. She didn't want to see Michi. But, more than that, she didn't want Michi to be sent away.

"Where are they going, Mama?" she asked, following her mother out the door.

"To internment camps in the Interior," Mama answered, hurrying them down the street. "Daddy didn't know exactly where. Apparently the government is building cabins. *Cabins*," she repeated scornfully. "I can just imagine."

"How long?" Jake said. "I mean, is it just for a little while? Or forever?"

Forever!

"I don't know. I don't think anybody knows. Till the war ends, I suppose." Mama's heels clacked on the sidewalk. "Oh, poor Fumiko."

• • •

Aunt Fumiko's eyes were red. Her cardigan was buttoned wrong; the bottom edge sagged below the last button. Esther had never seen Aunt Fumiko's clothing in disarray before.

Everywhere there were stacks of things: blankets, dishes, mittens, chopsticks. A trunk was open in the middle of the living room.

"Oh, Gladdy!"

"Fumiko!"

They threw their arms around each other.

"I don't want to leave my home," Aunt Fumiko said into Mama's shoulder.

"I'm so sorry," Mama said, patting her. Then she held her away. "No, I'm not. I'm furious. I'm so mad I can't see straight. I'd like to go to Ottawa and give the government a piece of my mind. How could they do this?"

Aunt Fumiko sniffled.

"Oh, I'm sorry," Mama said. "I'm making you feel worse. Here, what can I do? How can I help?"

Aunt Fumiko held out her hands. "I don't know where to begin. I don't know where we'll be living, or for how long. Or even when we'll be leaving."

"All right," Mama said, taking off her kerchief and setting down her purse. "Let's get started. You'll need warm clothes for the winter. Cooking utensils. Bedding."

Tomo, Michi and Akiko came into the living room. All three looked as if they had been crying.

Jake went over to Tomo. "Just when we were perfecting our secret play." His voice was thick. "And with the exhibition game in just a few weeks."

"Who knows if I'll ever play hockey again?" Tomo said.

"Don't say that!" Jake said.

"And I can't take my hockey stick, 'cause it won't fit into the luggage we're allowed to take."

"I'll send it to you," Jake said. "Once you get there, send me the address. I'll wrap it up in brown paper." He followed Tomo down the hall to his room.

"What a good friend," Aunt Fumiko said to Mama, smiling through her tears. Esther stood there.

"Come on, Akiko, let's finish packing," Michi said. She took her sister's hand and headed upstairs.

Esther followed. Michi hadn't invited her. But what else could she do? She couldn't stay in the living room. Then Mama would know for sure that something was wrong.

Michi won't kick me out of her room. Will she?

Suitcases were open on both girls' beds. Akiko's was half-full. Michi's was empty.

Esther stood by the door.

Michi handed Akiko an armful of sweaters. "Here, Akiko, pack these."

Akiko pulled a green sweater with yellow stripes out of the pile. "I hate this one. It's scratchy."

"Put it in. Mom said we have to bring warm things."

"No. I don't want to." Akiko dropped the sweaters on the floor and ran out of the room.

Without speaking, Esther picked them up, refolded them and placed them in the suitcase. Michi flicked her a surprised glance but didn't say anything. She opened the next drawer of Akiko's dresser and took out a stack of nightgowns, then handed them to Esther, who fitted them into the suitcase. She grabbed another handful of clothes.

"I wish you didn't have to go, Michi," Esther said in a low voice.

"I'll just bet," Michi said coldly.

"I mean it!"

"Well, you sure haven't been acting like it. But then, I guess you've been too busy playing princess dolls with Florence."

"And I guess you've been too busy playing hopscotch, and skipping rope, and collecting badges, and . . . and . . . everything else with Yoko and Noriko!"

"At least they don't ignore their friends," Michi shot back.

"You're the one who's been ignoring me!"

"You started it."

"I did not! And you were mean at Girl Guides," Esther said.

"Just because I had more metal than you—"

"Just because you showed off, you mean—"

The door opened. Mama and Aunt Fumiko peeked in. "Everything all right in here?"

"Fine," Esther and Michi said at once.

The mothers exchanged a look.

"Come on, Esther," Mama said. "We'd better go. I have to get dinner ready. We'll come back and help another time."

Esther shoved the pile of clothes she was holding into the suitcase. She turned and left.

CHAPTER 16

"Sit there, Elizabeth," Florence said, pointing at the window seat in her bedroom.

Esther sat Princess Elizabeth down. "I'm feeling a little peckish," she said. She bobbed the doll's head up and down. "Hey, I know. Let's raid the kitchen at Buckingham Palace. What do you say, Margaret?"

Florence looked as if Esther had suggested robbing a bank. "Oh, no, we might get caught. Let's embroider hankies instead." She moved Princess Margaret's hands. "I'm going to embroider a rose, Elizabeth. What are you going to embroider?"

"Uh, a dandelion."

"That's a weed."

"I like dandelions."

After several minutes of this, Esther said, "Hey, fancy going for a gallop through the woods on our horses, Margaret?"

Florence shook her head. "We might get leaves in our hair."

"Okay. Let's take the corgis for a run."

"For a walk, you mean." Florence walked Margaret sedately across her bed and back, moving a small furry stuffed dog at the same time. Esther followed with Elizabeth, left, right, left, right, slowly and regally.

They sat the dolls back down on the window seat. Just as Esther suggested, "Let's pretend we're dancing at our first ball," Florence rapped on the windowsill, making it sound like someone at the door. "Oh! Hear that? Our tutor is here. Time for lessons."

When she started putting Margaret through spelling words and sums, Esther stood up. "Sorry, Florence, I forgot I have to help my mama . . . uh . . . roll out pie crust."

And she would too, she vowed, even though she had never handled a rolling pin in her life and had no interest in learning how. Anything to get out of this.

"Right now?"

"Yes. The pies have to be done today. For . . . uh . . . a special raffle. For war orphans in . . . Belgium."

Stop! she told herself.

"Oh. Okay. Well, we'll play again soon. Farewell, Elizabeth." Florence waved Margaret's arm.

• • •

At home, Esther trudged upstairs. She started to put Princess Elizabeth on her usual spot on the pillow. She stopped.

Everything was ruined. The plan to get Michi the Princess Margaret doll was a bust, and Michi was still mad at her anyway, and Florence was bossy and boring, and if Esther couldn't play princesses with Michi, then she wasn't going to play with Princess Elizabeth at all.

She laid the doll in the box it had come in, and put the box in her closet.

. . .

At dinner several nights later, Jake said, "Did you hear? They're going tomorrow."

"Who?" Daddy said.

"The Suzukis. Tomo told me. They got their notice to be at the PNE at nine tomorrow morning."

"Oh, no!" Mama said.

So soon! Esther thought. The idea of Michi going away, as awful as it was, had seemed unreal, as if it might happen in some distant, hazy future. Not now. Not tomorrow.

Daddy slammed down his fork. "A bunch of us at the paper have been writing letters, trying to get the government to retract this crazy policy. But I guess it's too late."

"Where are they going, do you know, Jake?" Mama asked.

"Tomo said someplace called Kaslo."

"That's not far from Revelstoke, where Uncle Ted ended up," Mama said. "Do you think they'll let the men join their families, Herbie?"

Daddy shrugged. "Who knows? I guess that's something to fight for."

• • •

The next day, Mama and Daddy let Esther and Jake miss school, and the whole family walked over to the Suzukis' to say goodbye. The house was bare. Light-coloured patches on the walls showed where pictures had been taken down.

Aunt Fumiko's prized tea set, white with blue-and-red chrysanthemums painted on it, was gone from its place of honour on the dining room shelf. The mantel was empty of all the photos, figurines and hockey trophies that had stood on it.

Aunt Fumiko's mouth was set in a straight line, but when she saw Mama it wobbled. The women embraced, weeping.

As Esther stood in the living room, wondering where to go, what to do, she heard a thump. Michi was struggling down the stairs with a suitcase. Esther ran up the stairs. "I'll take that, Michi."

Michi held on for a moment, and Esther thought she wasn't going to let her help. Then Michi handed it over. "Thank you," she said politely.

"You're welcome," Esther replied in a calm voice, though all she wanted to do was cry.

Daddy fetched Aunt Fumiko's two suitcases from her bedroom. "Wait here, I'll drive you." He ran home to get the car.

Jake and Tomo wrestled the trunk and the remaining suitcases down to the curb. Mama and Aunt Fumiko followed, arm in arm. Jake and Tomo walked to the corner and back again, side by side, hands in pockets. Esther saw that Jake's nose was red.

Michi stood on the sidewalk with her suitcase, staring into the distance. Esther moved up beside her. "Michi, what's happening to you is awful."

Michi pressed her lips together. Esther knew that look. It meant that Michi was struggling not to cry. *I'm making it worse*, she thought, trying to think of something different to talk about. "Do you know where you're going?"

"A place called Kaslo. That's all I know."

"Maybe it'll be nice there," Esther said helpfully.

"I doubt it," Michi said.

"I didn't mean—" Esther began, but just then Daddy pulled up at the curb. He loaded the luggage into the trunk. Jake and Tomo shook hands, then, at the last moment, hugged. Esther grabbed Akiko and hugged and kissed her.

Akiko hopped into the back seat. Michi, without another word, without a glance, without a wave, climbed in beside her.

The doors slammed. The car drove away.

• • •

Michi's empty desk at school gave Esther a hollow feeling. She avoided looking at it, but her eyes kept being drawn in that direction, like a tongue probing the space where a tooth had fallen out.

The next day, Noriko's desk was empty. A few days after that, Helen and George Nishi left. Then Yoko.

More empty desks.

Frank Sakamoto.

Mary Takenuchi.

By early April there were no Japanese children left.

Trudy raised her hand. "Miss McTavish, where is everybody?"

Miss McTavish put down her arithmetic book and sat on the edge of her desk. "Can someone tell Trudy where our Japanese Canadian classmates have gone?"

"The government sent them away," Esther answered.

"Because they might be spies for Japan," Florence said.

"That's not true!" Esther said.

"My daddy says better safe than sorry," Florence said.

"And he should know, because he works in the war office."

Esther glared at her. *Of all the unjust, boneheaded moves,* she remembered Mama saying. She didn't think she'd better repeat that right now.

"It must be awful having to leave your home and go somewhere you've never been before," Ella said.

"And leave behind most of your things," Doris added.

"And your friends," Sam Goldberg said. He was best friends with George Nishi.

Miss McTavish stood. "Let's hope that the war ends soon and that, once Japan is no longer a threat, our classmates will be able to return. Now, back to our arithmetic lesson."

CHAPTER 17

eeks passed. Family after family of Japanese Canadians disappeared, bound for towns that Esther had never heard of: Greenwood, Lillooet, Sandon. One day houses were full with people coming and going, walking their dogs, weeding their gardens. The next day the houses were empty. Stores closed— Ota's Fish Store, Adachi's Shoes, Watanabe's Fashions, Nippon Variety.

Esther went with Mama to check up on Suzuki's Store. Mama had promised Aunt Fumiko to drop by every now and then to make sure everything was still in place.

The empty store, with cloths spread over the shelves, felt like a dead place. Esther remembered Aunt Fumiko slipping her the extra jawbreaker. She remembered customers chatting, the cash register ringing, Uncle Ted helping an elderly lady with her bags. She was glad when they left and Mama locked up again.

Back on the sidewalk, they turned at the sound of footsteps. Mr Harper was pointing at the CLOSED sign on the door. "Not a moment too soon, dear," he said to his wife. "Those Japanese could have been a danger."

"They were no danger at all, Mr Harper," Mama said. "And anyone who says so is spreading lies."

Mr Harper and Mrs Harper stared, open-mouthed.

As they walked on, Mama gave Esther a startled look. Then they both let out a nervous laugh.

• • •

Daddy continued writing editorials saying that the treatment of the Japanese was disgraceful. Mr O'Toole kept threatening to fire him. "But we're getting so many letters to the editor that circulation is up," Daddy told Mama.

Mama continued to bake. Every day the kitchen was filled with some new treat— muffins and pound cakes, brownies and butter tarts. The Red Cross raffled them off, and all the money went to war relief. People began to ask for Gladys Shulman's baked goods.

Daddy gained five pounds, but Mama stayed thin.

Jake's hockey team nearly disbanded, but then it combined with another team that had also lost players. Esther's Girl Guide troop did disband; there simply weren't enough girls to keep it going. She didn't miss it. It was no fun without Michi anyway.

At recess, Esther continued to trudge around the playground with Florence, picking daisies and braiding them into daisy chains.

"We're princess pals, right?" Florence said, placing a daisy crown on Esther's head.

"Mmphf," Esther mumbled. She hadn't told Florence she'd put her Princess Elizabeth doll away.

• • •

Grandma Sadie called. She announced that she was coming again, for Jake's birthday, in early May, two weeks away.

"Yay!" Esther said. Suddenly she longed for Grandma Sadie. "I can't wait. I wish you were coming tomorrow."

Grandma Sadie laughed. "Me too, *mommie-shainie*. But I'll see you soon. And I'll teach you to play Gin this time."

"Great!"

• • •

A letter arrived for Jake. The postmark was from Kaslo, British Columbia, and the envelope had been opened and taped shut.

"From Tomo," Jake said.

Esther, Mama and Daddy gathered around.

"Yikes," Jake said, scanning the letter.

"What?" Esther said.

"They're living in a shack. It has two small bedrooms and a kitchen. He says the bedrooms aren't much bigger than a closet."

"So much for building homes for the Japanese Canadians," Mama said, scornfully.

"They're lucky, though," Jake went on. "He says that some shacks have two whole families in them, five or six people in each room. They just have Uncle Ted's mom and dad in one room, and Tomo, Michi, Akiko and Aunt Fumiko in the other."

"Lucky!" Daddy began. "Of all the bloody—"

Mama put her hand on his arm. "Go on, Jake. What else?"

Jake turned the sheet over. Esther saw that some sentences were crossed out with heavy black lines.

"What's that, Daddy?"

"Government censorship."

"You mean somebody read Tomo's letter and crossed stuff out?"

"Exactly. So they can't tell us exactly what's going on."

"They have no electricity," Jake said. "Kerosene lights. A wood cookstove."

"Oh, my lord. Poor Fumiko," Mama said.

"They have to use an outhouse."

How embarrassing, Esther thought.

"Listen to this." Jake read,

"We're on a beautiful big lake, but even though it's supposed to get really cold up here, the lake is so big it doesn't freeze. So I won't be able to play hockey. But if you could send me my hockey stick anyway, I'd appreciate it. It would be like a piece of home."

"Herbie," Mama said. "What can we do?"

"Keep arguing. Keep fighting." He grunted. "O'Toole hasn't seen anything yet."

• • •

Esther went up to her room. Tomo hadn't said that Michi missed her. Or that Michi sent her love. Or even that Michi said hello.

Even so, Esther grabbed a sheet of paper and a pencil.

Dear Michi,

she wrote.

I am so sorry about what happened and I am so sorry that you have to live like that and I miss you and I still want to be your—

She stopped. Who was she kidding? Michi didn't want to hear from her.

She'll probably burn my letter without reading it.

Esther tore the paper into bits and dropped them into her wastebasket.

CHAPTER 18

"Grandma Sadie!" Esther flung herself into her grandmother's arms before she was even through the door.

"Esther," Daddy scolded, coming up behind with his mother's valise, "let Grandma Sadie get inside first."

"That's all right, Herbie," Grandma Sadie said. "My Estherle can jump on me all she wants."

Esther stood back to take a look at Grandma Sadie. She was wearing a pale blue felt hat whose brim sloped over one eye.

"Nice hat, Grandma."

Grandma Sadie grinned at her as she took it off. "It's very *au courant*, they tell me."

"What does that mean?" Esther said.

"It means it's made with currants," Jake said, coming into the kitchen.

"It does not!" Esther said.

Grandma Sadie laughed. "*Oy*, would you look at this beanpole. Come here, birthday boy, and give your *Bubbe* a kiss."

"Do I have to?" Jake said. He threw his arms around Grandma Sadie and lifted her off the floor.

"*Oy Gott*, put me down!" she shrieked. Then, when Jake obeyed, she winked and said, "Do it again."

• • •

Before dinner that night, Grandma Sadie, Mama and Daddy had another serious conversation in the kitchen.

Esther eavesdropped. She heard that Aunt Anna and Uncle Josef were probably still in southern Germany. Daddy had asked a colleague to check. At least there was no word of their having been shipped to a work camp.

At dinner afterward, Grandma Sadie was more like her old self. She teased Daddy about his growing bald spot. She ate two helpings of Mama's stuffed cabbage. "It's even better than my mama's, Gladdy, and that's saying something," she said, patting her middle.

She turned to Jake. "A young man like you must surely have a girlfriend," she teased.

"I do not!" Jake cried, though his cheeks turned bright red as he said it.

Esther made a mental note to grill him later.

It was good to have the real Grandma Sadie back.

· · ·

The next day was Jake's twelfth birthday. He had several buddies over. Some of them slapped Esther on the back like old pals; others awkwardly said hello in voices that squeaked one moment, growled the next.

The boys filled the living room with their big bodies and loud voices, jostling one another, faking hockey moves, teasing one another about girls and body hair, until Mama kicked them outside. They passed a soccer ball back and forth, their shouts rising up from the street, then crowded back inside and demolished an entire birthday cake, crumbs and all. Esther wasn't worried. She knew that Mama had baked another one for the family, safely hidden in the cupboard.

Jake's friends had chipped in together and got him new shin pads.

"Wow, fellas, keen!"

"Now for my gift," Grandma Sadie said, handing Jake a large box. It was new hockey skates, with stiff black uppers, pristine white laces and gleaming silver blades.

"A size big to grow into," Grandma Sadie said.

"Oh, Grandma, thanks! They're—you're swell!"

The boys laughed, clapped Jake on the back and shouldered out the door.

"Whew!" Mama said, collapsing on a chair. "Good party, Jake?"

"Terrific, Mama. Thanks." He sighed. "I just wish Tomo was here."

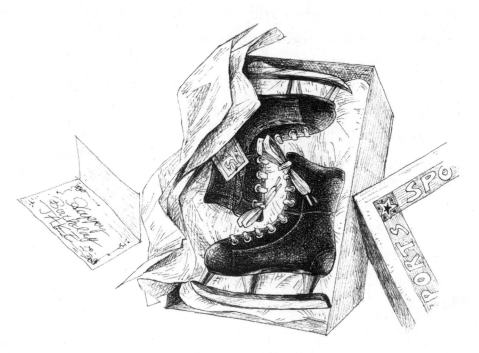

Me too, Esther thought, *and Michi too.*

• • •

After dinner, Grandma Sadie led Esther into the living room.

"All right, young lady, let's play cards."

Grandma Sadie explained the rules of Gin. "What you want is to get groups of cards that make a set, like this—" She put together the seven of hearts, the seven of diamonds and the seven of spades. "—or a run, like this." She fanned out the eight, nine, ten and Jack of clubs. "You see?"

"Mmm-hmm."

"Whatever you have left in your hand that doesn't fit into either a set or a run is called deadwood and is taken off your score. If you manage to get all ten of your cards into sets or runs, you 'go gin,' and you get a special bonus. Ready?"

Esther nodded.

Grandma Sadie dealt each of them ten cards.

What am I supposed to do? Esther realized that she hadn't been paying attention.

"You go first," Grandma Sadie said, nodding at the pile of face-down cards. Esther picked up the top card. Queen of hearts. She had a king of hearts. She couldn't remember what that meant, but she stuck the king next to the queen, just in case.

Grandma Sadie plucked a card. "Hmm . . . what to do, what to do." Smiling mischievously, she put down a card.

Esther drew and discarded. Grandma Sadie did the same. After her third turn, Grandma Sadie lay down her cards face up. "I'm knocking."

"Huh?"

"That means I'm putting out what I've got." She showed Esther her groupings. "One set and one run. So that's . . . thirty-six points, minus my deadwood . . . for a grand total of twenty-seven. What've you got?"

Esther fanned out her cards.

"Esther! You've got a run of hearts! Plus, three threes!" She counted under her breath. "That's forty points. Why didn't you knock sooner?"

"Uh . . . I forgot."

Grandma Sadie looked at her sharply. "You sure you're in the mood, Estherle?"

"Sure. No problem."

Grandma Sadie shuffled and dealt again. "Ooohh," she crooned, "looking good here."

They played several cards each. After Grandma Sadie's third turn, Esther sat there staring at her hand.

"Hello? Are you there?" Grandma Sadie waved a hand in front of Esther's face.

Esther managed a smile. "Yeah, I'm here. Uh, what am I supposed to do? Oh, yeah . . . " She drew a card.

"I go gin," Grandma Sadie said triumphantly, laying down her cards. "Two runs and one set. How about that?"

"Oh, well," Esther said, folding her hand.

There was a silence. Esther could feel Grandma Sadie's eyes on her. "Estherle, this isn't like you. You always play to win, and I have to keep my wits sharp. What is the matter?"

"Nothing, Grandma."

"Nothing, my foot. I've been hearing this . . . this *something* in your voice. What is it, sweetheart?"

Tears stung Esther's eyes. "Really, Grandma . . . it's nothing."

She went upstairs.

• • •

A short while later, there was a knock on her door. Grandma Sadie peeked in. "I just wanted to give you a kiss goodnight."

Esther opened her arms. Grandma Sadie sat on the bed.

"I see you still have all your Princess Elizabeth pictures up."

Esther nodded.

"I have more in my valise. I forgot to give them to you. I'll go get them." Grandma Sadie broke off. "Esther, where is your Princess Elizabeth doll?"

Esther lowered her eyes. "In the closet."

"In the closet? Why? Don't you love her anymore?"

Esther felt her throat get thick. "I love her more than anything." She burst into tears.

Grandma Sadie took Esther in her arms. "There, there, Estherle. It's okay. Let it out, *mommie-shainie*."

Esther sobbed on Grandma Sadie's shoulder. She didn't want to tell her grandmother what had happened, but somehow, with her face pushed against Grandma Sadie's chest, the story came tumbling out. "It was at our birthday party, when I got the doll." She sniffled. "I was so excited, and the other girls all gathered around me. And Michi felt left out, only I didn't know it." Esther wailed. "I forgot all about Michi—my best friend!"

Grandma Sadie didn't say anything. She just held Esther close.

Esther blubbered, then told Grandma Sadie the rest. How Michi had struck back by saying what she did at Girl Guides, and how Esther had come up with the plan to get the doll for Michi, and how it had fallen through, and how they had barely spoken to each other since. And how Michi had palled around with Noriko and Yoko, and how she, Esther, had got stuck with Florence, and how boring Florence was, and, worst of all, how Michi had left without saying goodbye.

"And I feel awful!" Esther said, bawling.

Grandma Sadie patted her back. She smoothed Esther's hair. Esther quieted.

"Oh, my Estherle," Grandma Sadie said.

Esther's eyes filled again. But her chest didn't feel so tight.

"Now," Grandma Sadie said, "I wonder what Princess Elizabeth would do."

Esther looked at her. "What do you mean?"

"Princesses always do the right thing, don't you think?"

Esther thought back to when she was trying to persuade Mama to get her the doll. What was it she had said? "Princess Elizabeth will set such a good example, I'll just *have* to follow it. You won't believe how good I will be."

Suddenly she knew just what to do. She told Grandma Sadie, and Grandma Sadie hugged her.

When Grandma Sadie left the room, Princess Elizabeth was back on the pillow. Esther smiled at her doll—her beautiful, wonderful, regal doll—and closed her eyes.

• • •

The next morning, Esther scrunched up several sheets of tissue paper, placed them in the Rafelson's box, and lay Princess Elizabeth on top. The doll's eyes closed with a soft click, but just before they did, they seemed to gaze at Esther with a warm look.

Esther placed more pieces of tissue paper on top of Princess Elizabeth. Then she took a sheet of paper.

Dear Michi,

She paused, pencil in hand. A dozen phrases floated through her head, a dozen apologies, a dozen pleas. But in the end, she simply wrote:

I am so sorry. Please can we still be best friends?
xox
Esther

She lay the note on top, closed the box, wrapped it in brown paper and taped it securely.

MICHIKO SUZUKI, she wrote, and copied the address from Tomo's envelope.

She carried the package to the post office. The postmistress smiled at her. "A care package for your friend?"

Esther nodded. That was exactly what it was. A *care* package for her friend.

She felt a pang when the package disappeared into a large canvas bag. But she skipped home, feeling lighthearted for the first time in a long time.

Then she waited.

❀ · · ❀ · · · ❀ ·

CHAPTER 19

"**Y**OU WHAT!" Florence shrieked.

She had just invited Esther over again to play with the princess dolls.

"I can't believe it," Florence said. "That beautiful doll will just get wrecked in that place."

"It will not!" Esther said. "Michi will take care of it."

"It's probably all dirty and muddy there."

"It is not." Though Esther wondered if maybe it was.

"And breaking up the set like that," Florence went on. "Princess Margaret here and Princess Elizabeth there. It's— it's not right."

Esther couldn't argue. It *was* a shame to separate the dolls. But then, since she owned one and Florence owned the other, they were separated anyway.

Florence put her hands on her hips. "It wasn't very nice of you, Esther. What am *I* supposed to do?"

"You know what, Florence?" Esther said. "I was thinking

about Michi, not about you."

"Well! If that's how you feel." Florence turned with a flounce and marched away. Trudy scurried after her.

Esther smiled. *Free of Florence.*

Doris ran by, chasing a ball.

"Doris?" Esther called.

"Yeah?"

"Can I play with you and Ella?"

Doris tossed the ball from one hand to the other. "I thought you were playing with Florence."

Esther grinned. "Not anymore."

"All right, then. Catch!" The ball sailed through the air.

• • •

Weeks went by. Another letter arrived from Tomo. He thanked Jake for the hockey stick. He said that his mom was finally getting the hang of cooking on the woodstove—"though we've had quite a few burned dinners," he added. He wrote that Aunt Fumiko and some of the other mothers were trying to get a school organized, but that it was hard because there were no classrooms, no desks and no books.

We might not have school this year,

Tomo wrote.

And you know something crazy, Jake? I miss school.

Esther shook her head. "That *is* crazy. I wouldn't miss it for a minute." Then she wondered if Michi missed school. But Esther didn't know, because Tomo didn't say anything about Michi. He didn't say that she was lonely or sad. He especially didn't say that she missed Esther.

• • •

Tomo's letter pushed Mama into action. She organized a campaign to collect books. She cadged worn-out books

from the library. She made the rounds of schools and talked teachers into handing over readers and math books and history books and science books. Esther and Jake went to all their friends' houses. People donated fairy tales and novels, comic books and cookbooks, books on astronomy and painting and horses. Soon Mama had eight cartons of books. Esther and Jake helped wrap the boxes in brown paper and address them and carry them to the post office. Esther was glad to help. She couldn't write letters to the editor. She couldn't shut down the camps. She couldn't bring the families back. But she could send books.

• • •

Another week passed. Still no word from Michi. No "thank you." No "oh, Esther!"

It's not very nice of her, Esther thought. *The least she could do is write and thank me.*

Then she had a thought.

She went to the kitchen. "Mama? How long does it take for a package to get to Kaslo?"

Mama spread a swirl of butterscotch frosting on a pecan bun. "Gee, I don't know. Not more than a week, I shouldn't think."

"A week!"

She stormed upstairs, barrelling into Jake, who was just coming out of his room.

"Whoa!" He put up his hands. "What's got into you?"

"I'm mad, that's what."

"Well, you don't have to take it out on me."

Esther frowned. "Say, Jake, how long did it take for Tomo's hockey stick to get to him?"

He shrugged. "Several weeks, I think. Seems like all the mail to the camps has to go through some government office."

"Several weeks?" That meant that Michi probably hadn't got the package yet. And then it would take more time for her to write back. She smiled. "Thanks, Jake!"

He stared at her. "Huh?"

· · ·

More weeks passed. Florence continued to snub Esther, and Esther considered herself lucky. She played with Ella and Doris instead. They skipped rope and played hopscotch and played tag. It was way more fun than walking around the playground with Florence, counting daisies and staying clean.

Jake's hockey season ended, and he started playing baseball.

Daddy wrote another editorial, this one saying that the government's seizure of the property of Japanese Canadian citizens, their homes and fishing boats and cars, was wrong. He received dozens of letters to the editor, most of them agreeing, but a fair many disagreeing, which had him spluttering in outrage for days. At least his boss, Mr O'Toole, had stopped threatening him. The *Vancouver Messenger* was selling like never before.

Mama continued baking.

And still there was no word from Michi.

She's the most ungrateful person who ever lived, Esther thought. *I'm sorry I sent the Princess Elizabeth doll to her.*

• • •

One day in late May, Grandma Sadie called. "Estherle!" she said. "How are you, *mommie-shainie*? Any news from Michiko?"

"No, nothing."

"Hmm. I wonder why."

Because she's rotten, Esther thought darkly.

"But I have some wonderful news," Grandma Sadie went on. "Is your mama there?"

"No, she's out delivering pastries."

"Oh. What did she make?"

"Apple-walnut cake with cream cheese icing."

"Yummm. Good thing I'm not there," Grandma Sadie, and she and Esther laughed.

"Is there a message?" Esther asked.

"Oh, I just can't wait to tell someone. Guess what, Estherle. Aunt Anna is safe!"

"She is? That's wonderful, Grandma. How do you know? Where is she?"

"She and Uncle Josef are in Switzerland. Oh, Esther, I've never been so happy. She phoned and said, 'Sadie? It's me, Anna,' only in German, of course. I thought, it's impossible, it's a hoax, it's a cruel trick someone is playing. But then she called me Schatzi, which was her nickname for me, so I knew it was her, and I burst out crying—"

Grandma Sadie let out a loud sob.

"Oh, Grandma!"

"I'm all right," Grandma Sadie sniffled, then laughed. "That's how I was, how we both were, laughing and crying at once, like two *meshugunas.*"

Esther laughed. "How did they get out?"

"It's the most wonderful story. A friend of Aunt Anna's helped them escape."

"How?"

"He knew someone who forged identification papers. So he paid to have fake papers made for Aunt Anna and Uncle Josef, and they crossed into Switzerland."

"That must have been scary."

"You bet. Anna said she was a nervous wreck going through the checkpoint at the Swiss border."

"That was really nice of the friend."

Grandma Sadie started crying again, softly this time. "May God bless him and keep him forever. He took a tremendous risk."

"Wow. It's like a miracle, isn't it?"

"Yes, Estherle. A real miracle."

CHAPTER 20

*T*he last week of school arrived. Miss McTavish kept the children busy with end-of-year tasks: cleaning out their desks, storing pencils and crayons and chalk in old cigar boxes, washing the chalkboards, clapping erasers.

"It's funny," Esther said to Doris and Ella, "if I had to do these jobs at home, it would feel like work. But doing them here is fun."

"I know what you mean," Ella said. "It's because we don't have to."

"And it's not our moms telling us to," Doris added.

On the last day, Miss McTavish asked the students what they were going to do over the summer.

Doris's hand shot up. "My family's renting a cottage on Vancouver Island."

"And I'm going with them!" Ella said excitedly.

"And we're going to swim."

"And go canoeing."

"And pick blueberries."

"Lucky," Sam Goldberg said. "All I'm doing is helping my father in his store. But I'll get to read lots of comic books."

The class laughed. Miss McTavish was constantly confiscating comic books from Sam, which he snuck from his desk when he was supposed to be doing work.

"I'm going to Girl Guides camp," Trudy said.

"That sounds like fun," Miss McTavish said. "Esther?"

"Nothing much," Esther replied. "Stay home, I guess. Read Nancy Drews."

Miss McTavish smiled. "How about you, Florence? Will you be going away?"

Florence shook her head. "My daddy's too important to take a vacation."

Esther stopped herself from pretending to throw up.

Just my luck, Esther thought. *Of all the girls, Florence is the only one who's going to be around.*

The summer stretched drearily in front of her.

. . .

On the first day of vacation, Jake went out to play baseball with his pals. Mama was making a rhubarb upside-down cake for another raffle. Esther chomped on a piece of rhubarb. She spat it into the sink. "Blech—sour!"

"Of course it's sour, you silly, it's rhubarb."

"Well, I didn't know," Esther said crossly.

She went upstairs and started rereading *The Hidden Staircase*, her favourite Nancy Drew book, but couldn't concentrate. Somehow, Nancy's quick wit and brilliant deductions irritated her today.

She took out her jacks and threw the pieces. She got through the onesies and was halfway through the twosies when the ball rolled under the dresser. She left it there.

Back downstairs, she started picking at a piece of cake batter that had dried on the kitchen table. *Chip, chip, chip.*

"What are you doing, Esther?" Mama asked, sliding the cake into the oven.

"Nothing."

"Well, find something to do. You're driving me crazy."

"I don't *have* anything to do," Esther said. "No one's around. All my books are boring. Jake's out. You're busy—"

The doorbell rang.

"Esther Shulman?" the postman said, holding a large package.

Surprised, Esther said, "Yes, that's me."

"Here you go, then." He handed her the package. "Looks like this nearly went around the world before it got to you." He pointed to four different postmarks. One said Kaslo, British Columbia. The next was smudged. Next to that was an ink stamp that said British Columbia Security Commission. And finally a Vancouver postmark. "At least it got here, eh?" He tipped his hat and left.

Esther looked at the return address. MICHIKO SUZUKI it said in neat printing.

Her heart leaped. *Michi! Michi's finally written to me!*

But what was Michi sending her? Another thought crept in. *What if it's the Princess Elizabeth doll? What if Michi doesn't want it, doesn't want anything to do with me, and is sending it back?*

Esther's face felt hot. Suddenly she was afraid to open the package.

"Who was it?" Mama called.

"The postman," Esther said, coming into the kitchen. "With a package for me from Michi."

"From Michi! How lovely. What is it?"

"I don't know. I'm going to take it upstairs."

In her room, Esther cut through the tape and tore open the paper. There was the Rafelson's box, the same one she had sent. Now Esther was sure that Michi was returning the doll.

Of all the mean, ungrateful, awful—

She opened the lid.

A folded sheet of paper sat on top of a layer of crumpled-up tissue paper. Esther unfolded it. Her mind was so full of thoughts that at first the words were a jumble. She forced her eyes to the top of the page and started again.

Oh, Esther,
Thank you thank you thank you!

"What?" Esther said. "So it's not—?"

I am so sorry too. I was rotten. Of course I still want to be your best friend. Forgive me?

Tears filled Esther's eyes.

You can't imagine how happy I was to receive the doll. I will take the best care of her ever, I promise. Of course I will give her back as soon as we get home (whenever that is). Until then, here is something I made for you (with a little help from Mom) (no, that's a lie—with a lot of help from Mom). I know that this could never, ever, replace your Princess Elizabeth doll, but I hope you will like it.

Esther, you are the best friend ever.
Love, Michi

Her heart pounding, Esther removed the crumpled tissue paper. There, on a bed of flannel, lay a doll. She was homemade, with a cotton face and round, stuffed arms and legs.

Immediately, Esther recognized her. *Princess Margaret*! Michi had made her almost exactly like the Princess Margaret doll from Rafelson's—the Princess Margaret doll that now belonged to Florence.

The doll wore a maroon sweater, that Esther recognized as an old scarf of Tomo's, and a navy, red and green plaid skirt—a school skirt of Michi's. The ruffle of white blouse that peeked out from under the sweater came from Aunt Fumiko's apron. Her soft feet were covered with black felt shoes, fastened by tiny buttons. Two small circles of pink cotton made her cheeks rosy. Brown yarn had been twisted into curls and sewn on all around her face.

Esther crushed the doll to her chest. She was homely and lumpy and a little worn-looking, and she was the dearest thing Esther had ever seen.

And Michi had made it for her.

She dug her cape out of the floor of her closet and put it on. She propped the doll on her bed. She dropped a curtsey. "Welcome to my humble abode, Your Highness." She placed her ear next to Princess Margaret's embroidered

red lips. "What's that you say? A slide down the banister? Yes indeed, do let's!"

Holding the doll by the waist, Esther ran in curves around her room, swooping Princess Margaret down the banister, up the stairs, down the banister again.

Panting, she stopped and held the doll at arm's length. "Not very ladylike, eh? But fun! And what's the use of being a princess if you can't have fun? Right?"

She bobbed the doll's head up and down. Princess Margaret's black button eyes were telling her something.

"Again? You want to do it again?" Esther laughed. "Your wish is my command, Your Highness." She pranced around, swooping the doll down and up, down and up. "Faster? All right! Here we go!"

Princess Margaret flew down the banister, turned a somersault at the bottom, and jumped up, arms outstretched. Her red embroidered lips curved upward in a smile—and Esther knew that the smile was aimed straight at her.

On December 7, 1941, the Japanese navy attacked a US naval base at Pearl Harbor in Hawaii. Immediately, the US and Canada declared war on Japan. In both the United States and Canada, people of Japanese descent were branded "enemy aliens" and quickly lost their rights. Both governments, advancing the argument that these citizens would be loyal to Japan and might share war secrets with the enemy, initially took away their fishing boats, cars, radios and cameras. Then in the spring of 1942, the Canadian and American governments began to remove Japanese people from the West Coast. In British Columbia, men between the ages of 18 and 45 were sent to the Interior to build roads. Women, children and older people were sent to internment camps, many of them in abandoned mining or logging "ghost towns." Small shacks were built to house them. These people lost their homes, businesses and possessions.

Over 21,000 Japanese Canadians were deported. Japanese Americans were allowed to return to the West Coast in 1945; Japanese Canadians, in 1949. In 1988, both governments formally apologized to Japanese citizens for the deprivation of their human and civil rights during the Second World War.

ELLEN SCHWARTZ is a highly acclaimed author of seventeen books for young children and teens, including several historical novels dealing with issues of social justice. She has written *Abby's Birds* and *Mr. Belinsky's Bagels* for Tradewind Books. Ellen lives in Burnaby, British Columbia.

MARIKO ANDO was born and raised in Osaka, Japan. As well as being an illustrator, she has worked as a printmaker and as a concept artist in the film industry. Her work has been exhibited throughout Canada, the US, Australia and Japan. She has lived in Vancouver BC, for many years.